THE GENTLEMAN'S DEMISE

J. B. Kelly

ISBN: 1493564366
ISBN 13: 9781493564361
Library of Congress Control Number: 2013920295
CreateSpace Independent Publishing Platform
North Charleston, South Carolina

DISCLAIMER

ACKNOWLEDGEMENTS

I am eternally grateful to my wonderful parents who gave me the courage and determination to accomplish my dreams.

I am forever indebted to my dear friend and editor, Kim Cherevas, who continues to support and assist me with my writing endeavors. She has the patience of a saint!

I would also like to thank my dedicated proofreaders, who took on the challenging task: my longtime friends, Camille Nebus, Helen Babits, Judy LaRocca and especially my sister, Ann Dunn. Their corrections and poignant suggestions are greatly appreciated.

I am again thankful and honored to have my signature book covers designed by the extremely talented Rory Sevajian Jr.

Lastly, I truly appreciate the good eye of Jennifer Hoyt Mayer and her last minute suggestions.

To Susie!

For my Irish Twin, Jackie

You are always in my heart!

I hope you
enjoy my sequel.
J. B. Kelly

God grant me the Serenity to

Accept the things I cannot change, the

Courage to change the things I can, and the

Wisdom to know the difference

BLAST FROM THE PAST

David lifted Patricia from her wheelchair onto the couch beside him and as he held her he stroked her hair while she continued to shake. "I am so proud of you, darling. I don't think I could have spoken to him and kept my composure the way you did." David grimaced a little and said carefully, "Although I would have relished the opportunity to talk to *him*!"

Patricia noticed the sharp emphasis on the word "*him*."

"You can say his name, David. I am long over Matt!" Or was she? The sound of his voice on the phone had an unexpected strong emotional effect on her. "I never could have gotten through this whole tragedy without you by my side. I actually feel so much better because I have closure to a very bad episode in my life. Now *we* can peacefully plan our future," she added, somewhat relieved.

"I only wish you hadn't mentioned the baby to him," he said sadly. He couldn't help worrying that their happy life could possibly be disrupted. He had worked so hard to win Patricia back.

"I'm so sorry, David, but I just wanted him to know how badly he left me. Don't worry, because now, as far as he knows, the baby died in that car crash. It's actually a miracle that I didn't lose him!" With that a wail came from the upstairs nursery.

"I'll run up and get that miracle child of ours," he said, taking the stairs two at a time.

Patricia sat thinking about how Matt duped her. She had gone over it many times before. How could she have saved herself from the claws of that creature? He was such a chameleon in that he managed to adapt to and manipulate every situation he encountered. And, boy was he good at it! So good, she never saw it coming. He was so loving and attentive to her. The memory of his touch still gave her a strange excitement. She remembered being attracted to his extremely good looks. He stood six foot three and had dark brown hair and those sexy "puppy dog" brown eyes. Despite that, she would never have gotten involved romantically or sexually with him had she known he was married. Regardless, she knew that she probably would have invited him to her house just out of kindness, instead of having him stay at a bed & breakfast with no electricity. That was just her caring nature. She felt that as terrible as it was that he never told her that he was leaving, the greatest violation was the cowardly way in which he left, without even saying good-bye. But enough about that stormy part of her life. She sighed. The rainbow eventually appeared with the love of her life, little Robby, at the end of it. And, in the end, she knew if it wasn't for Matt, she would not have Robby now. The baby made every bit of her excruciating pain, both physically and mentally, worth it. She reminded herself that she needed to separate the two emotions.

Patricia looked around the beautiful home that she had created with David. She had remained in the house after their divorce. It had always been her dream house. Her attention was drawn to the exact spot in this room where she and Matt had engaged in their first sexual encounter. I have to stop this right now, she berated herself. She needed to refocus on her life with David and Robby.

David entered the living room bouncing a giggling Robby on his arm. He was only an embryo when Patricia experienced her horrific car accident. Her doctor said that had she been any further along in her pregnancy Robby would never have survived. It was touch and go there for a long time, but Patricia's confinement to bed had added to his odds of survival. Looking at him now, no one would imagine that he was only three pounds when he was born during the end of the sixth month of her pregnancy. He remained in the neo-natal ward of the hospital as long as Patricia was detained there. Many expected him to have physical or psychological problems. However it turned out he was as normal as any other child and actually he excelled cognitively and his motor skills were advanced for his age. He was a charming child with dark brown hair and sparkling brown eyes. Unbeknownst to David, who'd never actually met Matt, the baby strongly resembled his biological father. However, Patricia refused to acknowledge any similarity and kept insisting the child looked just like her own long-dead father.

"Did you have a good nap, sweetheart?" she cooed to Robby as David handed him to her.

"I changed his diaper, honey, and I'll get his lunch while you play with him," David offered, smiling fondly at them.

Patricia and David had a long and complicated story. They had been married, but divorced more than six years ago when she caught him cheating on her with a younger woman at his office. At that time, they had been visiting a fertility clinic to no avail, and both of them were suffering from the ordeal. The treatments were painful and exhausting, and their bank account was being depleted at a rapid rate. The disappointments took a toll on their relationship. However, though she acknowledged that she had been quite moody and self-consumed at the time, she still felt it hadn't given him the right to violate their marriage vows. But that was an old pain resolved long ago, and they had since remained close friends and had fallen back in love with each other. It was David's steadfast devotion to her during the whole ordeal after the accident and the subsequent months of recuperation which convinced her of his sincerity. Now they had everything they had always wanted, including a baby. She couldn't afford to take a chance on losing the happiness that she had found for a fantasy lover. Later this year they were going to remarry. The race was on to see who would be able to walk down the aisle first, the bride or the ring bearer. That humorous thought brought her back to reality.

They decided on a small intimate wedding this go-round unlike their extravagant first. Patricia's parents spared no expense in order to provide her with a wedding befitting a princess. Patricia's father, Charlie, who had long passed, was born in Athenrye, Ireland and had come to Boston in his twenties in search of his "pot of gold". He thought he had struck the jackpot when he married Isleen Kelly, a Bostonian socialite whose father was the city's Chief of Police. Charlie was embraced by the Kelly family who helped him secure a job in the Boston Police Department. As far as Charlie was concerned, he had succeeded in obtaining the American Dream. Years later, Charlie couldn't have been more pleased when his only child, Patricia, introduced into the family her fiancé, David Callahan, a quiet reserved boy, also of Irish descent.

Patricia now began to muse on her and David's rather unusual first meeting, or perhaps better to refer to it as a confrontation. They each were at the Boston Common trying to flag down a taxi, both in a tremendous hurry to get to their destinations. They simultaneously converged upon a cab that was responding to the beckoning of one or the other. "Excuse me," Patricia said to David as they both grabbed the door handle, "but this is my cab. I signaled him first. Another will be along for you."

"Pardon me, miss, but I don't think so. He saw me first. Now please, I'm in a dire hurry and need to be somewhere in ten minutes," he insisted.

"Well that makes two of us," Patricia stated adamantly.

The two stood squabbling like obstinate children making a public spectacle of themselves until the driver, acting as referee, shouted over their noise, "Where are you going?"

The two answered as one, "Faneuil Hall."

"Well if the two of ye would stop the row and get in, I'll have ye there in less than five minutes," the diplomatic driver offered in his thick Irish brogue.

They quickly jumped in with Patricia hugging her door, so as to be as far away from David as possible. Lucky for him that we're going to the same place, she thought, because he wouldn't have gotten this cab over my dead body.

David, on the other hand, shrugged off the incident and extended the olive branch. "Hi, I'm David Callahan. Sorry about the misunderstanding, but at least it got sorted out."

Patricia hesitantly turned to him, saying softly, "I'm Patricia. I guess it wouldn't have been that intense if we both hadn't been in a hurry." She briefly realized that she was attracted to his subtle good looks with his curly light brown hair and his beautiful hazel eyes. She guessed he was at least six feet tall. She felt herself blushing and quickly turned her gaze away.

The driver interjected from the front. "I was just about to leave ye both bickering at the curb."

The two berated passengers looked at each other and broke into laughter over the silliness of it all. David insisted on paying the fare as Patricia thanked him and rushed out of the cab. The coincidence was compounded when they found themselves sitting two tables away from each other at the Faneuil Café. Patricia was dining with a longtime girlfriend, Nancy, while David dined solo, as though he had been stood up. When David sensed Patricia was preparing to leave, he quickly approached her table and asked if she wanted to share a cab back. Hence their life together began. Patricia hadn't known until much later that David had planned the whole episode in order to meet her. He was crazy about her from the first time he had seen her over a year ago, and had decided to take advantage of the opportunity when he saw her trying to hail a cab that day. Patricia was smiling at how naïve she had been back then. Yes, I know I've made the right decision by giving David a second chance, she thought. Her revelry was disturbed when David returned with Robby's lunch.

"He's such a good daddy, isn't he, Robby? You love your daddy, don't you?"

MATT REACTS

Matt stood in shock as he slowly hung up the phone after the troubling conversation he'd just had with Patricia. He felt a pang in the pit of his stomach. He had only called to tell her that he was back in the Litchfield area on another temporary work assignment, and he wanted to know if she wanted to get together. She had been so nice to him on his last stay eighteen months ago when he had been loaned to a local utility to help restore service after a nor'easter had devastated a good deal of the area. He had stayed with Patricia at her insistence and shared some memorable times with her, so she was one of the main reasons that he'd volunteered this time around. She had introduced him to some of her wonderful and interesting friends. He was looking forward to seeing some of them again, especially Dennis, the bartender at the Sahara, where Patricia was a waitress.

Maybe he should have told her that he was married and had a daughter, but the arrangement had been so short-lived. And maybe it was presumptuous of him, but it probably wouldn't have made a difference to her, or so he kept trying to convince himself. She was into him from the moment they met, his ego told him. He felt her strong attraction to him.

Alright, so maybe he should have said good-bye to her before leaving, but he had such a hard time with intimate partings. He thought it was ironic that for a moment he was able to identify with his father, who according to his mother had left them in the same cold manner.

Suddenly the events at the union hall earlier that day began to make sense to him. The fellows he had worked with so closely on his previous stint totally avoided him. Even Jack, his foreman, who had introduced him to Patricia, looked at him with intense disdain from afar. When Matt approached him, Jack completely ignored him. But his greatest disappointment came from Billy and Tommy, the two partners he'd worked with side-by-side for nearly a month. They literally turned their back on him when he walked up to them. He was treated like a scab that had crossed a picket line. Apparently, they held *him* responsible for Patricia's tragedy. What had made her go out and look for him in that terrible storm only to end in a horrific accident? The news that she had lost a baby, their baby, in that accident, made him feel nauseous, and he felt a sudden need for a drink. He started for the bar downstairs in his motel.

Matt was glad to find that he was not the only one sitting at the bar thus relieving him of any idle chit-chat with the bartender. He really didn't want to talk to anyone because he needed time alone to process his thoughts.

"I'm Tony," the bartender said as he extended his hand across the bar to greet Matt.

"Matt," he said distractedly, as he shook Tony's hand.

"What'll it be for you, Matt?" Tony asked cheerfully.

"Vodka on the rocks might help," he answered softly, and added, "no fruit please."

"Coming right up," he said, placing the drink in front of Matt. He was glad that Tony went back to the other end of the bar to resume his conversation with the only other patron who had been patiently waiting for his return. Matt noticed the lack of warm décor as he looked around the lounge. It certainly didn't offer the welcoming ambience like the bars he had frequented on his previous visit to the area. This bar had a cold and more austere atmosphere with its scratched wooden tables and chairs. The carpeting was a harsh brown color while the undecorated walls wore a faded ecru hue and were in desperate need of a coat of paint. The thought occurred to him that he was placed at this remote motel purposely; after all, his hotel last time was a beautiful bed and breakfast with all the warm amenities of home despite the lack of electricity. Maybe the character of this place would warm up with a couple of drinks, Matt thought with anticipation.

Matt's thoughts reverted back to that day eighteen months ago when he quietly got up from Patricia's bed so as not to awaken her and foil his fast get-away. He remembered taking a last look at her while she slept peacefully. It never occurred to him to have left any other way. He was sincerely fond of Patricia and maybe if he had not been married to his Katie things may have taken a different turn. But Patricia was well aware that their relationship was temporary. He just couldn't handle good-byes. After all, she knew he was on a temporary assignment and would be returning home at some point.

For the first time, Matt regretted leaving his roommate, Kevin, in the bed and breakfast when he decided to move in with Patricia for that month. Matt didn't even have Kevin for company this time because Kevin had not volunteered to come. After five drinks, Matt had absolved himself of any guilt, and he felt no remorse was necessary. He began to relish the memory of the homecoming party that Katie and his daughter, Laura, had thrown for him. He had walked into their apartment to find balloons flying and blow horns blaring. He felt like a military man might feel returning home after being abroad for a length of time. It was quite evident how much Katie and Laura had missed him. He loved his wife and daughter and couldn't picture his life without them. Laura had had a contract waiting for him to sign, in which he promised never to go away on business again. She had no idea that he was even in Connecticut now since she was away with her mother at the Jersey shore. Katie's girlfriend Ann Marie owned a summer home in Point Pleasant so they'd planned a girls' retreat for this week in order to keep Laura unaware of Matt's "breach of contract". He began chuckling aloud at the thought.

His reverie was interrupted when Tony placed another drink in front of him. "It's on me, Matt. It's last call; I'll have to ask you to drink up," Tony said, yawning, obviously ready to call it a night.

"Thanks," said Matt, barely coherent at this point. He gulped down his drink and staggered out of the bar. Tony watched him go, and felt just a little bit sorry for him.

The next night Matt was back at the bar in the same seat. Tony wasted no time and had Matt's drink ready as he sat. "Good memory you have there, Tony," Matt said.

"It comes with experience," Tony answered politely.

Tonight there were at least five other people who were also sitting at the bar but were involved in their own private conversation, so Tony focused on Matt. "Are you from around here?" he asked Matt. Tony noticed that Matt was still in his work clothes from the previous day. He knew Matt was staying at the motel because he was charging his bar tab to his room. He thought maybe Matt and the wife had a spat and he needed a temporary abode.

"No, I'm from Jersey. I'm on loan to a local utility union for five days. I thought I might be staying longer but that won't be the case." He sighed.

"That bad, huh?"

"Worse than you can imagine. I expected to socialize with some of the people whom I met the last time I was here, a year ago last October," Matt said. He was almost quivering, very much like a sad little boy. "I just like to have company. I'm not the loner type."

"Well, what happened? Did they all move away?" Tony asked facetiously.

"No, it's just a big misunderstanding. Anyway, I have only two more nights left in this work week," he said in relief. "Come Friday afternoon, I'm out of here." Tony was signaled over by the other patrons who were in need of replenishment. Matt was grateful that Tony didn't ask what the misunderstanding was all about. He wasn't sure that he could explain it properly without creating more confusion; especially since Matt himself wasn't sure *he* really understood what exactly had happened.

After a couple more drinks, Matt stumbled his way to his room to sleep off his alienation. Only two more nights like this and I'm going home to my two girls…that was his last thought as he drifted off to sleep.

> *He knew that he had been sleeping but for how long he had no idea. It could have been five minutes or five days for all he knew. A loud crack of thunder had startled him awake. Struggling to process his surroundings, Matthew groped aimlessly in the dark trying to identify where he was. He could easily feel the boundaries of his enclosure at the ends of his elbows. It was a very tight fit. The loud thunder clapped again causing him to jump and knock his head against the back wall of the confine. He began to shake with fear and was filled with panic. He realized that he was still locked in his bedroom closet, or as he thought of it, his nightly coffin. It had been his mother's only means of childcare while she worked the graveyard shift for the last two years. She couldn't afford a real babysitter. His breathing rapidly increased with each heavenly rumble. He became paralyzed with fear causing him to relieve himself in the diaper his mother forced him to wear. He began crying for his mother, the only person who could free him from this frightful prison. He could*

now hear the rain pounding on the roof above.
The booms of thunder were occurring more often
along with the other eerie sounds heard during a
severe storm. It was an explosive roar that shook
the house and caused Matthew to bolt upright...

When he looked up at his bed from the floor, still panting, Matt realized with some relief that he was back in his motel room. The sparsely decorated room looked a lot less dismal to him now, after that brief retro nightmare experience. Matt remembered how he incessantly begged his mom to let him remain in his bedroom while she was working. She insisted that she couldn't take chances and needed to know that he was not in harm's way. She constantly reminded him that the reason they lived this way was because his father had abandoned them. She would then go on to tell him it was not her fault. Not her fault at all. This diatribe only served to confuse him, and even now, he could not come to terms with his mother's abusive, illogical behavior.

He was desperate for a drink, but the bar downstairs was long closed. He would have to remember to pick up some vodka on his way back from work tomorrow. Just two more nights, he told himself over and over, only this time he didn't doze off. He was sorely afraid that he would again be locked in that dark 'coffin' of a closet.

CHAOS

Matt was disappointed to say the very least when he found no one home to greet him. It was a far cry from the celebrity's welcome that he'd received upon his last return from Connecticut. He poured himself a drink to relax while he waited for Katie and Laura to come home. He had a fleeting impression that Katie had improved on her domestic skills. Her lack of house-cleaning abilities had always been a huge complaint of his. He "relaxed" himself into a drunken sleep after finishing off a quart of vodka. He awoke to Laura shaking his shoulders, and calling with excitement, "Daddy, Wake up! We're home!" Flailing his arms in alarm, Matt pushed Laura so hard that she fell to the floor.

Katie ran to help her up. "Are you all right, honey?" she asked, as Laura broke into sobs from the shock of her father's rejection. Katie's reaction as a protective mother kicked in then, and she shot him an angry look and shouted, "Matt, what on earth possessed you to do that?"

"She should know better than to shake someone awake," he snapped, causing Laura to wail even louder. Katie gently steered Laura into the bedroom and tried to soothe her daughter's hurt feelings before she returned to berate Matt.

As she entered the living room, he shouted, "Where were you?"

"Have you lost your damn mind?" she screamed back, unable to comprehend his awful behavior. She made a step in his direction and spotted the empty vodka bottle at his feet which only confused her more. "Where did this come from?" she asked as she bent to pick it up.

"I put it there, and you didn't answer my question!" he shouted. "I asked you where you were!" He tried to stand but fell back awkwardly onto the sofa.

"You're very drunk!" Katie said, a little shocked to hear herself saying it, since she'd never seen Matt this way.

"If I am, it's your fault!" he accused. "You should have been home instead of running around. I shouldn't have had to come home to a lonely, empty apartment," he said, spitting his words out angrily.

She found herself raising her voice in self-defense, "I took Laura to the pediatrician for her annual checkup, if you don't mind!"

"I do mind! You weren't here when I came home after being away for a week!" he seethed through his teeth.

"Matt, what is this all about? Did something happen in Connecticut to upset you?" Katie was trying to calm down, but she wasn't even sure how to feel right now. She was still angry but also concerned about the present situation.

"Nothing *happened* in Connecticut," he said defensively, trying to distance that place from his mind as he fell back and passed out again on the couch.

She went in to Laura's room now and found her lying on the bed in tears. "Laura," she whispered softly, "I think it would be a good idea for you to go stay with Grandma for a few days. Let's pack a little suitcase for you and I'll bring you there now."

Laura's grandmother always enjoyed her visits. Laura liked to stay with her not only because she loved her, but also because she lived next to Suzie and Ann Marie. Ann Marie was Katie's childhood girlfriend. She had moved back into her mother's house after her divorce from Rory, who she'd caught cheating. Now Ann Marie's daughter Suzie was Laura's best friend. The girls were born a day apart in the same hospital and had stayed extremely close.

As they were leaving the apartment, Laura said that she forgot something and ran back in. She had remembered that she never left home without giving Matt a kiss and a hug. But she abruptly stopped and hesitated a few feet from her sleeping father; she thought better of it, and decided to blow him a silent kiss instead. While walking to her mother's house, Katie tried to soften Matt's tirade. "Laura, I think it'd be a good idea that we keep what happened today to ourselves," she suggested. "You know Daddy didn't mean it. He was having a nightmare when we woke him up before. He'll be back to himself when you come home," she said in a reassuring tone, although she wasn't sure she believed that. "We wouldn't want anyone to think Daddy was bad, right?"

"Mommy, Daddy never yelled like that at me before," she said as her voice quivered. "I just wanted to give him a kiss and hug, but he pushed me away."

"I know, honey. He was just having a very bad dream at the time. I'm sure he is very sorry," she said, trying to convince herself as much as Laura.

Matt's behavior earlier had been surreal. What would make him drink a whole quart of vodka causing him to act so crazy, she thought? She was hoping Matt would sleep it off while she was out. She certainly didn't want to experience an encore of their earlier episode. He had better have a good excuse for his vile behavior.

Katie stayed at her mom's a couple of hours while she settled Laura in before returning home. She didn't want to rouse her mother's concern over a stupid incident, so she let on that she and Matt needed some time alone after his absence. Her mother, like everyone else, held Matt in high esteem, believing him to be the epitome of a gentleman. She didn't want to tarnish that image. Katie sincerely hoped that Laura would keep their secret.

Katie was worried when she arrived back home and found Matt was not there. She couldn't imagine where he could have gone. She had just about finished sorting his dirty clothes from his clean ones when he staggered into their bedroom. "So you did it again," he shouted at her. "You left me alone. I wanted you so badly," he slurred" as he lunged toward her and pushed her down on the bed. She couldn't possibly wiggle her tiny body from under his dead weight. He forcedly took her face into his grimy hands and tried to kiss her, but she resisted, and turned her face away so his mouth caught only the side of her head. He tried again but she kept shaking her head from side to side. "I want you, Katie, I've missed you all week." His words were slurred and his breath reeked of stale vodka. Katie found herself feeling disgusted at the thought of him, something she never would have believed she could feel. This was Matt, her charming husband, to whom she never said no, but the thought of any intimacy with him now made her want to vomit. Matt became uncontrollably enraged by her rejection and he slapped her across the face so hard that her nose began to bleed profusely. He lifted himself off her for a sobering moment at the sight of the blood and the awareness of his own violent behavior. He slowly staggered back towards her apologizing, "Katie, I'm so sorry. I didn't mean it."

She glared at him as she sat up and ordered him, "Get out! I want you out of here now!"

He regained his balance, turned his back in shame and began to leave. He looked back at her once more, and ruefully murmured, "I am so sorry, Kates."

After Katie heard the front door softly close, she flopped back onto the bed and cried for hours. What had happened to her Matt?

"Matt hasn't been the same since he came back from Connecticut this time," Katie told Ann Marie with great concern. She couldn't hide his bizarre behavior anymore, and she needed to confide in someone.

"What makes you say that? He's been home for a couple of months now," she said, confused.

"Ann Marie, he wasn't even gone a whole week this time, but I'm telling you that there is something different about him. Something happened in Connecticut to cause this change. He's been drinking every day since he came back. Laura doesn't understand why she doesn't see him, and I don't know what to tell her. She's at my mother's again this week, I keep thinking it's best for her not to be near him." She took a deep breath. "Ann Marie, he slapped me."

"He what?" she cried in disbelief. "When? Why?"

"It was right after I got back from taking Laura to my mother's and he had returned while I was sorting laundry on my bed. He was drunker and even angrier…he forcibly pushed me onto the bed…I thought he was going to rape me." Katie started sniffling at the memory. "When I rejected him, he slapped me." Even though the pain from the slap Matt had inflicted had not lasted, in her mind she could still feel it as if he'd just done it.

"I've never known Matt to do anything like that!" Ann Marie said, incredibly shocked at her friend's admission. "He's always been so gentle and loving," she added.

"Exactly!"

"Have you said anything to him about how worried you are?" questioned Ann Marie, now concerned for her friend.

"He becomes snippy and accuses me of nagging when I say anything," said Katie on the verge of tears. "He actually pinned me up against a wall earlier in the week in front of Laura and…" but before she could finish, the front door opened and in sauntered Matt, obviously intoxicated.

"Hello girls," he called loudly. "And how are you two beautiful ladies doing this fine night?" he asked as he headed for the liquor cabinet.

"Matt, do you realize what time it is? You never called or came home for dinner," Katie exclaimed. "I've been worried sick about you!"

"Now Katie, we have a guest, so mind your manners," Matt said as he gave her a quick glare.

"Ann Marie, I hope you don't mind but I think I'll go to bed. I've come down with a nasty headache. I'll give you a call in the morning," Katie said quietly so as to avoid an argument with Matt in front of her friend. She quickly left the room.

"Ann Marie, would you like to join me for a drink?" Matt asked. He started pouring one for himself just as though nothing was wrong.

"Maybe I'll have a glass of red wine," she answered. She was hoping that she might be able to help Katie out if she could get Matt to confide in her, having now witnessed for herself the change in his usual demeanor.

As he handed her the wine glass, he touched her face with his other hand. "You know, you really are an attractive woman, Ann Marie," he said in an intimate manner. She started to feel extremely uncomfortable. Matt had never spoken to her this way. He was always the perfect gentleman. Maybe she had made a mistake in thinking she could help. Maybe another time when he was sober might be better, she thought nervously.

"Oh wow, I didn't realize it was this late," she said as she glanced at her watch. "I'm sorry Matt, but I'd better be going." She put down the wine and reached for her coat.

"Here, let me help you with that," he said as he held her coat for her.

As she turned in to her coat, he grabbed her by the shoulders and kissed her ferociously on the mouth. Ann Marie was stunned and desperately trying to push Matt away, as he tried to part her lips with his tongue. The bizarre moment was interrupted with a gasp, followed by Katie shouting, "What the hell is going on here?" She turned to see Katie standing there with a look of fire in her eyes. Ann Marie was finally able to push away from Matt, who seemed not bothered in the least by the whole incident.

Ann Marie pleaded with Katie through the bedroom door, "Katie, please let me in. It's not what it looked like. I would never do anything to hurt you! Katie, please let me in!" She could hear Katie sobbing uncontrollably on the other side of the door. Ann Marie's heart was now breaking for Katie, and she started crying too. After a while she thought it better just to leave it until tomorrow; besides, she wasn't even sure what she could possibly say. She herself was terribly upset by Matt's behavior. Right now, Katie was incapable of listening to her anyway. "I love you Katie," she called to her through the door.

Ann Marie marched up to Matt in the living room and slapped him across the face as she shouted, "How dare you!"

"You've always wanted me," he said, matter-of-factly.

"Are you serious? You've always been like a brother to me! Katie is my best friend!" she shouted incredulously, not able to believe he could possibly accuse her of wanting him that way.

"Oh, she'll get over it," Matt said as he staggered across the room and fell back into his easy chair. A moment later, he passed out. Ann Marie knocked on Katie's door. "Katie, he's asleep. Please come out and talk to me." There was no reply, just the sound of Katie softly sobbing. Ann Marie thought it was best to just leave at that point.

Extremely upset, she cried all the way home. She had grown up with Katie and couldn't imagine life without her. She had to convince Katie of her innocence. Now she began to understand the "drunken Matt" poor Katie had been dealing with. What had become of the Matt they knew? She had always known him to have impeccable manners. She was as disgusted with Matt as Katie had apparently become, but now her only concern was repairing her relationship with her best friend.

In the morning, Matt awoke to find his bags packed by the front door with a note that read: *Don't call me or contact me. I've had enough! These last few months have been hell. I will communicate with you only through my lawyer. As for Laura, I want what is best for her and you are not that right now. GET HELP!*

She didn't even sign it, he thought. She can't be serious! I was only teasing Ann Marie, he told himself. She can't possibly hold me responsible for anything more than having a few too many drinks, he further convinced himself. This was all her fault from the start. All right, maybe a break from each other may do us good. She'll be begging me to come back. Anyway, she can't keep me away from my daughter.

Ann Marie answered her front door to a pathetic sight. Katie was standing there with her hair unkempt and swollen red eyes from crying all night. Ann Marie wasn't sure what the purpose of this visit was until Katie fell into her arms crying hysterically. They both fell to the floor sobbing. "Katie, you know that I would never do anything to hurt you," Ann Marie spoke sincerely.

"I know. I saw you pushing him away. I couldn't believe that he would try something like that with you, my closest and dearest friend. I told you that he changed since he came back from Connecticut. He goes to the bar every day after work. He's going to lose his job if he continues this behavior. He's developed a severe drinking problem and I don't know how to deal with it."

"What are you going to do?" Ann Marie asked as she slowly disentangled herself from Katie and stood up. Katie remained on the floor with her back against the wall.

"Well, I kicked him out and told him to get help. I have to play hardball with him to get my sober Matt back." Her voice cracked. "In the meantime, I need to find a job and someone to watch Laura."

"I can take care of Laura, so don't worry. Maybe the consistency of seeing Suzie and me every day will ease her separation anxiety from Matt. She also has your mom and dad right next door here. The girls love to visit with them."

"But I don't want them to know anything about this yet. Why upset them over a hopefully temporary estrangement?"

"And Katie, I was thinking, a talk with Father Seamus might help. He counsels people with drinking problems. In fact he runs the local AA program. He might be able to give you some advice. It's worth a try."

"Oh, Ann Marie, what would I do without you?" Katie cried, as she threw her arms around her lifelong friend. "This week is going to be so difficult. I don't know what to do first." Then, somewhat irrationally, she added, "Would you please call Bowla-Bowla for me and tell them that Matt and I won't be bowling this week? I really don't want to talk to anyone right now."

"Of course I can make a call to the bowling alley. Don't worry about trivial things like that now. Is there anyone else you need me to call? You know, Katie, you've always been there for me when I needed you. And I will be here for you now, whatever you might need. I guess that's what best friends are for." She helped Katie up from the floor and held her again as they both cried some more.

MATT'S NEW PLAYGROUND

Matt looked around at his temporary abode, a room at the YMCA. It wasn't much larger than a jail cell although it did resemble one, minus a toilet which here at the Y was located down the hall and shared by all his floor mates. He wasn't particularly keen on his new surroundings, but it would have to do until Katie came to her senses. He certainly didn't plan on staying in this lonely, depressing place for too much longer. He was happy that he had been able to secure the last available room.

Although he was exhausted after working all day, he became antsy looking at the four walls and felt a claustrophobic episode coming on. The episodes were recurring childhood flashbacks of when his mother had locked him in that bedroom closet.

He remembered that tonight was usually his and Katie's date night which they typically spent bowling together. He contemplated going to the lanes, but decided that he had better not in case she might be there. He certainly didn't want to run into her. She might think that he was looking for her. No, he wanted her to come to him and beg for his forgiveness. He felt the sudden urge to be around people so he decided he'd go out to grab something to eat. Matt had a constant craving for companionship because of those haunting memories of his childhood. He was delighted to find a quaint Irish pub around the corner from the YMCA. He took a seat at the bar and waited patiently for the bartender to take notice of him.

There was a lively crowd sitting around the bar engaged in jovial conversation. From the crowd's playful banter, and the way they seemed to be enjoying each other's wit, Matt deduced that they were all regulars. He was quite content with his new find. The barman made his way down the bar to him with a broad smile.

"And what will it be that you'll be havin'?" said the barman with a thick Irish brogue.

"I think I'll try a black and tan," Matt replied.

"That it'll be," said the man.

It took a minute for the Guinness to settle before the fellow topped it off ever so cautiously with Harp lager, so it layered to make the obvious colors of black and tan. He proudly placed his creation on a coaster in front of Matt who was now salivating at the sight of his drink. It will be a pleasant change from vodka, he thought.

"Thank you, sir," Matt said.

"I haven't been knighted yet, so it'll just be Kieran to ye," quipped the barman with a gleam in his eyes.

"And I'm Matt, the knight in shining armor who fell off his horse."

"Oh, so you've gotten yourself in trouble with the missus, have ye! I'm only out of the doghouse meself," Kieran replied with empathy. "There's no figuring women, I tell ye."

"You can say that again," Matt wholeheartedly agreed. Kieran noticed some other patrons' drinks were near empty, and went to refill them leaving Matt alone with his thoughts. It was a short thought though, before an attractive strawberry blonde stood beside him. He was not aware that she had been watching him from the moment he had walked through the bar's door.

"Hi, I'm Nicole, but my friends call me Nikki," she said in a very sweet, yet provocative tone.

She immediately captured Matt's attention, since she sported tight black spandex pants with neon green stilettos, accenting the low-cut lime colored blouse that emphasized her well-endowed bust. It was hard for him to talk to her without fixating on the obvious attraction. She seemed to enjoy his attention.

"You don't mind if I sit here, do you?" she asked, and sat before he could even answer.

"I'm not good company right now," he said trying to be polite. The last thing he wanted to do was complicate his life with yet *another* woman. Isn't that what turned his happy life upside down in the first place?

The vixen continued on, "I hear that misery loves company. Maybe we can be miserable together," she coyly suggested.

Matt was aroused by her sensual behavior. She lifted her wine glass delicately to her red glossed lips as she sipped her drink. That's a sexual gesture, he thought. Oh no, he had to stop this now.

"I really don't want to seem rude, but I'd like to be alone right now. It's nothing personal but I need quiet time."

Disappointed that she had not made a new conquest, Nicole lifted her glass to him as she toasted, "To better times." She then rose from her barstool and intentionally stood close enough to him so that her breast rubbed against his chest. She whispered, "If you change your mind, I'll be waiting." Matt became aroused as he watched her wiggle back to the other side of the bar. She's some hot number, he thought. Katie had just better hurry and come to her senses. I can't take being alone like this for very long. He sat and drank until he was sure he'd be able to fall into bed and hoped he could sleep without having any lucid nightmares.

It was last call before he knew it and time to go back to his lonely cell. Kieran made his way over to say goodnight. "As much as I'd like seeing ye again, Matt, I hope ye make it up with the wife. Speaking from experience, son, the drink is a lonely partner who offers a lot of empty promises."

"It's the only solace I have right now, but thanks for caring," Matt answered, and he walked out the door.

"I see ye haven't made up with the missus yet," Kieran said to Matt as he approached the bar the next day, this time with a friend.

"No, she hasn't come to her senses yet," he replied in an unexpected cheery tone. "I'd like you to meet a good friend of mine, Kevin Gillen," he said as they took a seat.

Kevin mused to himself, I walked through the bar door his coworker, and now I'm his best friend? How did I ever let him talk me in to coming out tonight?

"Glad to meet ye, Kevin," Kieran greeted him warmly. "So what has you out with himself tonight?" he asked, nodding at Matt. He sensed that Kevin must have been coaxed somehow to accompany Matt.

"Matt here assured me a night of good Irish humor," Kevin answered.

"Ye'll indeed find it here," he said alluding to the boisterous crowd gathered at the bar.

Kevin stood at six feet with a head of soft, blonde curls and tranquil blue eyes. He was thirty-five, single, and unaware of any sex appeal that he might possess. Women found themselves more attracted to his reticent demeanor than he realized, although he generally disregarded their attention. Some years ago Kevin was literally left at the altar by his fiancé of five years. He still bore the scars of rejection by the one woman he had truly loved and cherished.

"What can I get for ye tonight?" Kieran asked.

"Two black and tans please," answered Matt.

"Great Irish ambience, huh, Kev?" Matt asked with pleasure, obviously proud of his newly discovered playground.

"It does have traditional charm. It reminds me of the pubs back home," he agreed, smiling as he glanced around at the dark wooded walls with Celtic designed windows. The walls sported paintings of thatched cottages and Irish patriots. There were also lilting ballads playing in the background, ensuring the appealing authenticity of the pub.

"So, fellas, where are your people from?" Kieran asked the two, whose facial appearances boasted the map of Ireland.

Matt was the first to answer, "I really don't know my genealogy," he pensively answered, as though he was thinking about it for the first time. "My father left when I was young, and my mother never talked much of her ancestry. I slightly remember my grandparents having brogues, but they died when I was young."

There was an awkward silence and they both looked to Kevin for his response. "I was actually born in Belfast but we moved when I was two. My father was Protestant and my mom Catholic." He paused, and then went on to say, "They wanted to escape the troubles". He was of course referring to the constant discord between the Catholics and Protestants in Northern Ireland. "They first settled in Connecticut because one of my grandmothers was originally born there. She later went back to Ireland, only to return to America years later with my parents. We eventually moved to Hoboken when my da got a job on the docks here."

"I'm from the New Lodge Road in Belfast meself," Kieran answered, happily enjoying the kinship he felt talking of home.

"We hear that things are quiet there at the moment but we never know what silly notion will ignite the tinderbox," Kevin said, starting to relax as the conversation progressed.

"Unfortunately that's a perpetual row that will never cease," Kieren asserted.

Kevin asked him when he had last been home.

"Last year I went to a cousin's wedding." Kieran started to talk about his extended family, and obviously wanted to regale them with a tale about the aforesaid wedding, but he was interrupted.

"Kieran, our throats are parched over here," a spokesman for the crowd called to him.

"Don't get your knickers in a twist," he answered playfully, as he started towards the other end of the bar.

"Well, Kev, was I lying when I said this was a great place?" Matt said. "What were the chances you'd meet someone from your hometown, let alone the bartender!" Matt felt sure that Kevin would be his constant companion at this place.

"Yea, what a coincidence, I really do like it here," he replied, looking at Matt with sincerity. "But look here, I didn't know you and your wife had a falling out," he added, genuinely concerned.

"I'm enjoying the break from our usual routine." Quickly, he added, "she'll be begging me to come back any day now."

"Just don't let it go on too long," Kevin warned him, "I'd hate to see you lose a good thing and not be able to get it back." He quickly changed the subject so he wouldn't come across as being preachy. In any case, this had no effect on Matt, who was eyeing up the bar for action. "Did you work with the same guys this time in Connecticut?" he asked referring to the fellas that Matt had worked with almost two years ago.

"No I didn't," Matt answered abruptly.

"I thought you would have stayed at your foreman's house again."

"Foreman's house?" Matt asked, confused. Quickly, he realized that he had told Kevin that he'd left their shared room in the bed and breakfast to stay with Jack, his foreman. Of course, Kevin knew nothing about Patricia and the real story.

"Oh no, this time was much different and my assigned work crew wasn't as hospitable as the one before."

"What happened? You, your foreman, and those two great guys you worked with the first time were so tight!"

Matt appeared agitated and unintentionally snapped back, "No, it was very different this time." He was unaware that he had piqued Kevin's interest.

"I'm sorry to hear that. Did you at least get a chance to see them while you were there?"

When Matt didn't respond to him, Kevin took the opportunity to lighten the obviously tense moment. He loved the song that was playing and decided he felt like dancing. His impromptu performance of Irish dancing brought a crowd and in no time, they were clapping him on and singing to the Irish ballad. They cheered for an exhausted Kevin at the end.

"Here ye go, on the house, Michael Flatley," Kieran teased as he put a black and tan in front of him. "That was a good show of the Horn Pipe ye did thar."

"Wow, nice job, buddy," Matt said, obviously impressed at Kevin's show of talent.

"I have to hit the bathroom, I'll be right back." Matt stood up, happy that the Irish ballad had put an end to Kevin's previous inquisition.

He left Kevin to wonder about Matt's abrupt change in behavior in response to his innocent questions. Why wouldn't he think that Matt would have returned to the same work crew as the first time? After all, they had been so good to him while he was there. They put him up, fed him, took him out and they even lent him their car to return to Hoboken twice. Something must have gone terribly wrong somewhere, but Matt made it quite clear that he had no intention of discussing it.

Meanwhile Matt used his visit to the men's room as an excuse to end their conversation. The last thing he wanted was to dwell on Connecticut. After all, Kevin had no idea that it was Patricia and not Jack that he had moved in with for that month, he thought to himself as he made his way back to Kevin at the bar. He tried to push it further and further back in time. His disturbing thoughts were interrupted by Nikki's seductive greeting, "Hi, there, handsome. I see you brought company with you tonight. Do you mind if I join the both of you?" she purred, nodding towards Kevin.

"Sure," he answered her, welcoming the distraction from his and Kevin's previous topic of conversation.

Kevin didn't know what to think when Matt returned with a woman that he apparently knew already. The woman was not in the least modest in her dress and she wore a tight body forming miniskirt that just about covered her rear end. This was paired with an extremely low silver sequined top and stilettos that matched. His immediate impression was that she was a cross between a barfly and a prostitute, and he, Kevin, wanted nothing to do with her.

"Kevin, I'd like you to meet Nicole, she likes to be called Nikki." Matt surprised himself that he actually remembered her name from the night before.

"Hi," Kevin answered, obviously not happy about the intrusion.

"Hello," she murmured close to his ear, brushing against him as she seated herself on the barstool next to his. "You sure can dance."

Kieran started toward them rolling his eyes in warning at Kevin, who looked back at Kieran as if to say "What the hell?"

He stood up and backed away from the bar, saying, "I'm sorry Nicole, but I'm just leaving." He had no interest in entertaining the likes of her, and his actions spoke as much to Matt.

He shook hands with Kieran and assured him that he would be back to see him again. He turned to Matt and said, "I'll see you on the job tomorrow, buddy." He really didn't want to leave Matt alone with Nikki, fearing that Matt was falling fast from grace. Women like Nikki have been destroying marriages for years, he thought, a bit judgmentally. He hoped Matt wasn't vulnerable enough right now to fall prey to her seduction, but decided it was best for him not to get involved any further.

KATIE'S INNER TURMOIL

Katie felt like a nervous school girl as she stood waiting in the small dimly lit foyer of St. Ann's rectory. Although the beautifully crafted dark mahogany paneled walls added to its austerity, tiny stained glass windows on either side of the vestibule provided much needed small rays of colored light. In a weak moment of angst Katie considered running out, but she had already announced herself to the person on the other side of the intercom. Besides, she had called earlier that day and made an appointment to see Father Seamus. Her second thoughts were beginning to impair her common sense. Oh, why did she listen to Ann Marie? Why was she here? An inner voice took over, "because you need help. You have to think about Laura!" She began to anxiously pace back and forth in the small confines of the rectory vestibule.

The heavy wooden door was gently opened by Father Seamus and Katie was immediately put at ease with his broad welcoming smile. "C'mon in, Katie," he said as he held the door for her.

"Hello Father. I hate to bother you. I'm sure you are busy with more important matters."

"Kathleen Reilly, you *are* important," he said as he led her into his office. As he started to pull back a chair for her, she suddenly broke down in sobs. He patiently waited until she calmed down and the sobs became sniffles, then handed her a tissue and with a quiet gesture indicated the chair. "Please sit down," he said, as he left the room. He quickly returned with a glass of iced water and placed it on the table within easy reach. Instead of sitting across from her, he pulled up a chair next to her, angled it towards Katie, and sat down.

"Now Katie, tell me what is causing you such distress and making you so unhappy."

Katie took a deep breath and began relating the whole wretched story beginning with Matt's latest trip to Connecticut, and the visible change in his behavior upon his return. She told him about Matt's progressive drinking, and the unprovoked verbal and physical abuse. An extremely embarrassed Katie cried as she told the priest how Matt brutally attacked her the night he had returned. She stressed to the priest that up until now Matt had never mistreated her or their daughter and that he had been more of a social drinker; that was, until his return from Connecticut a few months back.

Father Seamus sat and listened attentively to Katie as her eyes misted with each traumatic revelation of the events of the past month. She looked at the unassuming priest and desperately said, "He's like a tortured soul who won't share his pain with me. What can I do?"

He pensively paused before he answered, "Nothing, but pray and put this in God's hands. It's too great for you to handle alone. It appears that Matt has developed a severe drinking problem. Is there a history of alcoholism in his family?" he asked. "Despite controversial opinions, alcoholism is a disease that is usually but not always genetic."

"No, I only know that his dad left him and his mother when he was a toddler, and that his mom had to fend for them both with no monetary means or family assistance. I've never met any relatives other than his mom. Matt never talked much about his childhood or his life before I met him. I do know that his mother was angry and bitter about the dismal events of her life and tried to inflict that guilt upon him. But again, Matt never talked about it. I observed it for myself after we were married, when he took on the responsibility of his mother's care until she passed away."

It never occurred to her that Matt could possibly be an alcoholic. "But Father, Matt was always a social drinker. He could take it or leave it," she said slowly, and then continued, a bit uncertainly, "I really don't understand what could have happened."

"Katie, *that* is one of the biggest mysteries of the disease. It affects each of its victims differently. It can be triggered by their first, hundredth, thousandth … drink. There is no rhyme or reason to the illness. But when it takes hold, it becomes a lifetime rollercoaster ride. There are only three ways off, stop drinking, hit rock bottom or death. The only cure is abstinence."

Katie looked at the priest horrified. She confessed to her overwhelming guilt of throwing Matt out of their home. He took her hand, and emphatically said, "It's Matt's decision to stop drinking, and there is nothing you can do or say to stop him. Do you want to expose Laura to a perpetual life of dysfunction and disappointment?"

"No of course not, but I feel so helpless," she said, exasperated. Looking the kindly priest straight in the eye, she asked, "Father, does this mean my marriage is over?" By now, her voice was quivering and the tears were threatening again.

"Not at all, Katie! Alcoholics have an extremely selfish alter ego, especially when we drink. It becomes all about us and our drinking. Nothing and no one else matters. If Matt submits to being powerless to the disease and seeks assistance from God and fellow alcoholics, he can resume a normal life, but only with the complete abstinence from alcohol. Until he comes to that realization, you need to prepare for a future without him. Many alcoholics lose their jobs, their families, and ultimately their lives, because they choose not to seek help, or are just incapable of it. I am a recovered alcoholic. I suffered many humiliating travesties because of my alcoholism, until nineteen years ago when I sought help with the grace of God. That is why I've become a great advocate of Alcoholics Anonymous." Katie was a little taken aback by his personal confession, and didn't really know how to respond to this humble priest from whom she had been seeking answers, so she remained silent.

"But, Father, I still think Matt's drinking is because of something that happened in Connecticut," she insisted.

"Katie, there usually is an underlying excuse that alcoholics use for their behavior, once the disease has taken hold of their lives. But then there are choices to be made. They can deal with whatever is causing them to want to drink, and try to correct the behavior, or they can continue to drink, perpetuating the pain for themselves and their loved ones. You are a strong woman and now you must make decisions for your future as well as Laura's. I would strongly suggest that you and Laura attend Al-Anon meetings, so that you will have group support."

He reached over to his desk as he said, "I have some information here about alcoholism, AA, and Al-Anon. It may help give you some insight into Matt's affliction. In order for AA to help, Matt has to work the program centering on the twelve steps. They are listed in the brochure. One of the later steps is for recovering alcoholics to make heartfelt amends to everyone they hurt during their drinking career. It is necessary for them to purge their guilt by revealing their indiscretions, and to genuinely apologize for any hurt they have caused."

Katie thanked the priest for his time and invaluable advice, and assured him that she and Laura would see him at Sunday Mass. Katie felt overwhelmed by Father Seamus's revelations. She agreed that she needed to make major changes in her life and in Laura's. She couldn't be guaranteed that Matt would stop drinking; therefore, she would look for a job and she would try to ease Laura into adjusting to life without him. In her mind, she implored God to remove this cross and cure Matt, who was the only man she had ever loved.

The walk home from St. Ann's gave Katie time to process the advice Fr. Seamus had given her. Could Matt truly be an alcoholic? Katie didn't want to accept that. She decided not to discuss any of this with Laura until she herself better understood it.

She stopped at Ann Marie's to pick up Laura, and was glad to find the little girls were busy playing dress-up in another room. It gave Katie the opportunity to relate the details of her meeting with Father Seamus to Ann Marie.

"I don't like the idea of this roller coaster ride Father Seamus talked about. I feel like Matt pulled me on with him, but I need to get off, Ann Marie. It's moving too fast and the dips are so frightening. Matt's drinking is destroying my life"

She acknowledged that Matt had always been a very clingy person. They'd always spent all their free time together or with Laura. They both enjoyed belonging to their weekly bowling league. It was true that he was always with her except for when he went to work, or when she and Laura went to weekly Mass. It saddened Katie that Matt didn't have any interest in God or developing a relationship with Him. He had grown up without any faith identity, and his mother never encouraged any because she was too busy indulging herself in her own bleak and empty pity pool. Katie wondered how and if Matt would take to AA and its deep-rooted foundation in submitting to a Higher Power.

Her thoughts changed to the present, "I need to prepare a plan for a new life for Laura and myself in case Matt doesn't recover," she said, and started to weep hysterically. "I need to stop and get today's paper so I can start looking for a job. It's been so long since I've worked, other than at being a wife and mother. I'm not sure if I am qualified for anything else."

"Katie, of course you are! What about your bookkeeping experience? You did it until you had Laura and you free-lanced for a time after. I'm sure you haven't forgotten that," Ann Marie said, trying to reassure her friend.

Katie's thoughts wandered back to when she and Matt had attended college. He took some electrical courses at Steven's Institute which helped him land his job with the local utility company. She graduated from the local community college, having been granted a two year business degree with a concentration in accounting. She was now sorry she hadn't pursued her B.A. and C.P.A., but still, she was grateful to be able to fall back on the education and experience she did possess. "I really want my old life with Matt back," Katie whimpered. "I miss him so much."

"Would you take him back now, the way he is, and sacrifice yourself and Laura to his drunken abuse and humiliation? Which, by the way, will only get worse with time and your enabling," Ann Marie said emphatically. "C'mon, Katie, you have to be realistic."

Katie stopped crying. She wiped her eyes and gave Ann Marie the semblance of a smile. "No, I couldn't...I know you're right, I have to wait until he comes to his senses. I pray nothing happens to him, Ann Marie. I really wouldn't be able to bear it."

"Listen Katie, granted, Matt is a very sick man, but only he can control his illness. You are not putting that drink in his hand and forcing him to drink it." But before she could finish, the two little girls wiggled and wobbled into the kitchen wearing oversized high heels while modeling Ann Marie's dressy wardrobe. The mothers giggled at the sight. It was a much needed reprieve from their previous topic.

"Hello Mother," Laura said imitating the voice of an adult socialite. "It's so good to see you, darling," she added.

Suzie continued the charade with the same sophisticated tone, "It was so nice of you to drop by, dear Katie. It's always a pleasure to see you."

The two girls strutted around the kitchen entertaining the women until Laura lost her balance and fell into Suzie, causing them to both to land on the floor. The mothers were in stitches laughing, as the two Mademoiselles rubbed their bums and pouted in humiliation.

"I think you both need to polish up on your modeling skills," Ann Marie quipped as she lifted Suzie from the floor and Katie raised Laura. The four of them fell into a group hug as they reveled in the silliness.

"Mommy, can we go with Suzie and Ann Marie to their shore house for a few days?" Laura pleaded.

Katie looked to Ann Marie for help. She couldn't go to Point Pleasant at a time like this. She knew how much they all enjoyed their "girl time" there but it was out of the question for the time being. Her life as she had known it was crumbling around her.

Ann Marie quickly saved the day, saying, "Katie, you have a lot of things to do in the next couple of days, so why don't I take the girls myself?"

"That would be great. Of course, I would rather be with you girls, but I made appointments that I have to keep," she said apologetically. The next few days would give her time to organize what she could, enabling her to have a heart-to-heart talk with Laura about their new living situation. She wasn't looking forward to that chat, but she knew it couldn't be put off much longer.

"Okay, Mommy, I need to go home to see Daddy before we leave. I have to remind him to take care of Mattie for me. I miss them both so much. Why does Daddy have to work so much? I never get to see him anymore.

"I don't see him either," Katie said trying to be a bit truthful with her daughter. Can't you call his boss and tell him I need my daddy?" Laura said this so innocently, and her words tugged at Katie's heart. Laura had no idea that her father wasn't living at home anymore. She had been spending all her time at Ann Marie's and at her grandmother's. Every time she'd asked, Katie had told her he was working.

"Honey, he's working very late tonight," Katie lied again. "I know how you feel. I miss him too. Hopefully, this is only temporary and doesn't continue too much longer. I'll remind him about Mattie for you." As soon as this lie escaped her lips, the full weight of how things had changed really hit her, and she almost lost control again.

"Okay, but tell him I owe him lots of kisses when I see him." A look of relief replaced Katie's panicked look. She was just grateful that she was once again able to prevent Laura from learning about the true reason for Matt's absence. Katie started thinking about all the times she'd witnessed the sweet father and daughter relationship between Matt and Laura. The memories of Laura's playful affection toward her father now made Katie's heart ache even more.

NEW DREAMS

"David, I was thinking maybe you *should* expand the partnership, and take that new position in New Jersey. Moving would give us a brand new start as a family. What are your thoughts?" Patricia asked, cuddling Robby as he giggled, seemingly in agreement. She looked down at her son. He was getting so big and in the last few months was becoming steady on his feet. He was also talking up a storm. She and David both felt he was incredibly advanced for his age.

"I was checking around the area of Montclair where the new office is opening," he said, thrilled at her interest. "I really liked the neighboring town of Cedar Grove. It was somewhat similar to this neighborhood." He quickly added, "I really think you might like it too." Patricia had a minor flutter of panic thinking that Cedar Grove might be close to Hoboken where Matt lived. She quickly calmed her own fears by remembering that her physical appearance was drastically changed after her life-altering accident. She had hoped that he would never recognize her now. She lost count of the many plastic surgeries she had suffered through to attain her new face. She now sported short dark brown hair opposed to her previously shoulder length auburn hair. The only natural feature that remained the same was her beautiful hazel brown eyes. She felt like a person in the witness protection program. Feeling reassured, Patricia turned her attention back to her two admirers.

"Would you like to take a ride there today?" David said, as he prepared to take the baby from Patricia in order to feed him.

"Do you want to go for a ride in the car?" she asked Robby as he bounced on her knee. He gave her a big smile and repeated "car", pointing to the door.

The impromptu trip to New Jersey was an enjoyable Sunday drive for the Callahan family as they cruised down I-95 with Robby "eewing" and "aahing" at any passing vehicle that was bigger than a car.

"Wook! Ruck!" he exclaimed pointing to each in a childlike excitement.

His parents were grateful that he fell asleep less than a half hour into their ride. Just after crossing the George Washington Bridge, they followed the Route 3 signs to Route 46 and then onto Cedar Grove.

"You were right, honey, I do like this area," Patricia told him. Her "alter ego" was asking her if Matt's unexpected call some months ago might have initiated a subconscious draw to New Jersey on her part. She tried to suppress these thoughts. It still hurt her to think about Matt.

They rode around the town of Cedar Grove and stopped at a local restaurant, The Celtic Match. David scooted out of the car with an energetic flare and in no time had the wheelchair out of the trunk, opened and ready. He pushed it around to the already opened passenger door, and gently lifted Patricia as she wrapped her arms around his neck and he placed her in her temporary means of transport. Once he had her comfortable, he lifted a squirming Robby from his car seat and placed him in Patricia's lap. The happy family headed to the wheelchair ramp at the side entrance to the pub.

They enjoyed the Celtic ambience as well as the menu. "I haven't had good Irish food since we last went to Boston how many years back," David exclaimed with excitement as he savored his bangers and mash. "I don't know about you, but this place is enough to make me want to move here." After David had wheeled his sated wife and son out of the pub and had gotten them situated in the car with the wheelchair back in the trunk, they decided to explore a little more of the Cedar Grove area before heading on to the new office in Montclair.

They liked the neighborhood around the reservoir the best, which they later learned was called Ridgewood Acres. It was set off from the rest of the town by surrounding dense woods. Patricia jotted down the real estate numbers on the signs outside homes that were up for sale. She was excited about calling them the next morning.

They took note of the lovely church St. Catherine's that they would probably be attending. It was situated on a corner property with rolling knolls of green lawn. Its location added to the small town's attraction. The Callahans continued traveling up the steep winding road which led into Montclair.

They were fascinated by the huge homes and mansions that boasted "old money."

"I'd hate to have to clean that house," Patricia said in exasperation as they passed a ginormous house standing on acres of property.

"Just as I wouldn't want to have to mow its lawn," David laughed.

"Well that takes care of that, no mansion for us," Patricia offered with a chuckle.

After a further two minute ride toward the main part of town, they came upon David's new business domain. It was a two story gray-bricked building with large dark tinted windows. It wasn't long before David began his routine of getting both of his charges situated, one in the wheelchair and the other one on Patricia's lap. Patricia was relieved to see the handicap ramp leading to the back entrance.

"I'll be glad when I can walk by myself," she said. She so desperately wanted to relieve David of the burden of caring for her and Robby. She was determined to walk before the wedding, which was still nearly a few months away. Her dedicated physical therapist, Keith, encouraged her persistence on a daily basis in order to make it possible.

"Darling, I would carry you to the ends of the earth," David answered earnestly as he looked down at Patricia with tremendous love and devotion. She smiled back at him with the same sentiments.

Once inside, Robby toddled over towards the desk and climbed up onto David's office chair. He fidgeted around until he was able to kneel on the chair as he reached for the phone.

"Hewo," he called into the telephone as he held it upside down. "I, Wobby," he informed his imaginary caller. "I work-in," he continued. "You firet," he shouted into the earpiece of the phone, and then awkwardly put the receiver down backwards. David and Patricia were amazed at his adorable behavior. They realized that he must have picked up that lingo from *The Apprentice*, a TV show they sometimes watched. "What a little sponge you are," David said to him as he sat down and lifted Robby onto his knee, cuddling and kissing him as he giggled.

"So what do you think?" He looked at Patricia, as he continued tickling Robby.

"I think that we should rent out our home in Connecticut just in case our venture doesn't work out," she suggested, "but I am definitely more comfortable with the idea of moving after seeing the area. Let's start making plans tomorrow!"

SECOND CHANCES

The tiny white clapboard chapel with its steeple pointing toward the heavens faced the spacious village green. Beautiful arched stained glass windows depicted biblical stories in colorful mosaics, while its large double oaken doors harbored an abutting alcove which gave the holy haven its welcoming charm.

The landscape was meticulously groomed by a group of parishioners, and bloomed in a painted variety of extraordinary colors. The flowering dogwoods, daffodils, roses and other springtime blooms showered the grounds in heavenly hues – picture perfect for a wedding. Patricia was happy they'd be able to have their wedding pictures taken on these gracious grounds, instead of at the gazebo across the way on the village green. She wanted to leave her Matt memories there, preferring to identify with the rebirth of the spring blossoms on the church property.

Inside, the church was abuzz with whispers of excitement as the guests awaited the start of the wedding march. This ceremony had become the event of the year for many in this small Connecticut town. Several of David and Patricia's friends and relatives were gathered to witness their nuptials. Most of them had accompanied the couple on the long painful journey which brought them back together today.

"How I prayed for this day," sniffled Patricia's mother, Isleen, dabbing at her eyes with a tissue.

David's mom, Elizabeth, nodded in agreement. She said softly, "Me too."

David's dad gently chastised them, "If you two keep up this behavior, you'll have the whole church boohooing!"

"Oh Robert, we can't help it! We're just so happy for Patricia and David getting their second chance at happiness!" Elizabeth professed. Robert rolled his eyes at the response from his spousal drama queen.

The other guests were busy admiring the modestly decorated sanctuary. Two gold vases of cream colored roses stood at the foot of the altar. There were bows of ivory attached to each end of the sturdy oaken pews, ten on each side of the main aisle, softening the austere look. The deep rich red carpeting in the sanctuary area extended into the nave and the transept of the small church, giving it a royal appearance.

"This church is just gorgeous," whispered Roz to Marie as they waited anxiously for the ceremony to begin. The two women were seated with their husbands, Bob and Charlie, who were quietly making their own observations.

"It really is," she softly replied. "I see a lot of familiar people here," she added, as she turned and glanced around the church.

Roz, trying not to act as obvious, questioned, "Anyone I know?"

"Surely you know the sisters, Marilyn and Maggie, the two from the Sahara who were so good to Patricia when she was convalescing after her terrible ordeal."

"Ladies," Bob interjected, in a firm but quiet tone, "I want to remind you that there is to be no talk at all about 'The Gent' today."

"That's right," Charlie affirmed.

The two men were making sure their wives' conversations didn't veer onto the off-limit topic of "The Gent", the facetious code name they used when referring to the dreadful Matt.

"We wouldn't dream of committing such a sacrilege like that today," miffed Marie.

The simple church bore a modest but regal décor. An impressive handcrafted crucifix hung above the marble reredos, the large altarpiece attached to the back wall of the sanctuary. Two saintly gilt-trimmed reliefs were affixed to the walls on the outside periphery of the sanctuary. The only ornate fixture in the church was the Holy Tabernacle placed behind the altar on the center of the reredos, which attracted the congregation's attention.

"This is a really pretty little church," Sue whispered to John. "It's so intimate, don't you think?"

"I never liked big ostentatious churches anyway," answered John, louder than he realized.

His daughter Danielle who was sitting behind him, overheard. She leaned forward and whispered in his ear, "Daddy, I love this church. I want to have my wedding here too."

He turned his head and playfully said to her fiancé Sean, "I'll pay you to take her off my hands!" Danielle rolled her eyes as she nudged her dad in the back. Others around them chuckled with the welcomed distraction.

Their other daughter Amanda and her husband Nick were expecting their first child any day now and thought it better to stay home. They wanted to be closer to their hospital in case Amanda were to go into labor.

Seated a couple of pews back, Marilyn had thoughts of her own, as she turned to Maggie and asked, "Do you see David? I don't see him at the altar. Do you suppose something has happened?"

"Oh, really Marilyn, he'll probably step out of the sacristy when the wedding march begins," she snapped, a bit sharply, Marilyn thought.

It was at that precise moment that the music began and all rose and turned towards the back of the church to watch the pageantry begin. The altar server led the procession carrying a cross, followed by Father Charles and the Rabbi walking jointly down the aisle.

The whispers began, "I didn't know either David or Patricia was Jewish." Patricia's mother was quick to explain quietly to those around her that "Rabbi and Mrs. Rabbi" as Patricia called them, had been two of Patricia's favorite lunch regulars at the Sahara. They had volunteered along with others for her round-the-clock care. They had opted to be part of the overnight team of caregivers. Rabbi had meant a lot to Patricia so she asked if he would do her the honor of reading from the Old Testament, since she and David chose not to have a Mass but just the marriage ceremony. The Rabbi assured her that it was he who was honored, and would be pleased to do the reading at her wedding. When he offered to give an additional marital blessing in Hebrew after their vows were made, Patricia and David gladly accepted.

There was a slight pause and then the wedding march began as Patricia was escorted up the aisle not only by David but also by little Robby; they were all walking. No one had expected this sentimental display of family unity, so there wasn't a dry eye in the church as the three slowly made their way to the altar. Patricia, though limping, looked brave and radiant. She was clearly in some pain, as she clung to David's arm. David allowed himself a glimpse of Patricia in profile and thought how amazing it was that she was walking up the aisle with him. Three weeks ago when she'd first stood up from that wheelchair and took a dozen tentative steps across the living room, he saw her resolve and knew she would be here beside him today. Little Robby wobbled just in front of them. It still amazed Patricia to see Robby walking since he'd only just taken his first steps a few months ago. He was dressed in a toddler's tuxedo as he confidently teetered up to the altar determined not to fall, occasionally looking back to be sure his parents were following *him* – their fearless leader.

Patricia leaned into David and whispered. "This is even nicer than our first time around."

"That's because you don't have to worry that I won't be waiting at the altar," he answered discreetly, smiling at everyone, as they slowly made their way.

She tugged his arm as she declared, "I love you, David Callahan."

They both exchanged doting looks on Robby as he stole the show by waddling up the aisle and smiling away, as he waved the ring bearer pillow all about. David was relieved that Patricia had had the sense to pin their new wedding rings to it.

"Where did she ever get that beautiful dress?" Lynn asked Alexa in a hushed tone. "I know she was worried about finding one that would cover all of her scars."

"It's so elegant," Jane chimed in. "Looking at her now, who would even imagine she had any scars?" She added, "Well, except for the limp." Lynn shot Jane a look, thinking that it hadn't been a very sensitive thing to say, even though Patricia's limp was still obvious.

"She's wearing her original wedding dress," Theresa informed them. "She had it preserved, and then wasn't able to part with it after the divorce. She was delighted to find that it actually still fit her."

"I don't think that I could be so lucky to fit into mine," sighed Lynn.

"Would you ladies please zip it?" Chris asked, trying to be polite, feeling like all this scrutinizing of Patricia was getting to be a bit much.

Patricia had found the dress at a vintage shop in Boston years ago. It was ivory in color, an A-line dress with a high lace Victorian collar and long billowy sheer sleeves.

When the couple and their toddler finally arrived at the altar, Patricia's matron of honor, her best friend Nancy, and David's best man, Jack, stepped out of their pews and joined the three. Jack took Robby's hand and lifted him into his arms.

"Good job Buddy," he praised his godson. The two had practiced their parts so that Robby would know what to expect, to ensure he would act appropriately. Robby loved his Uncle Jack and did not want to disappoint him.

The ceremony was beautifully performed by both clergy as whimpers and sniffles came from the congregation. Loud applause followed the pronouncement, "Announcing for the second time, Mr. and Mrs. David Callahan."

"This time is forever," announced David publicly as he scooped Patricia up in his arms and carried her down the aisle. The recessional hymn of celebration resounded as they were followed by Nancy and Jack, with a beaming Robby between them.

Patricia was not able to endure a receiving line at the church, so the wedding party and guests headed immediately to the Sahara where the reception was being held.

The small banquet room was decorated beautifully for the quaint occasion. Long stem lilac and ivory flowers in tall silver vases were on each of the six tables which were set up along the periphery of the dance floor, three on each side. The D.J. had a compact setup in a corner of the room, and the banquet bar was set in a small recess in the wall next to the entrance at the head of the dance floor. The main ingredients for a fun celebration were in the mix.

Dennis, the professional, along with Billy and Tommy, two of his usual bar customers, had gladly volunteered to bartend for the occasion so that each would have an opportunity to enjoy the party also at some point.

"You two can cover for me when I need a break," Dennis told them. He wasn't sure how the comedy duo would do behind the bar, since they were dangerous enough sitting on the other side drinking. Billy and Tommy were two of Jack's local utility men who always frequented the Sahara, and they had become very close to Patricia while she waitressed there. They had worked directly with "The Gent", and were as stunned as everyone else at the outcome of his departure. The two had been uncharacteristically serious during those rough days after Patricia's accident. Today, with the happy occasion, they were back to their old ways and their comical energy fed off each other naturally, always resulting in unexpected entertainment.

"Everyone should be on the way so maybe we could open the champagne, and put the glasses on the table for the toast," Dennis suggested.

"Sure, I'm good at this," Billy enthusiastically agreed, as he watched Dennis expertly place a bar rag over the bottle and twisted it until the top subtly popped. His two apprentices tried to follow suit as Billy fumbled with the rag, twisting the top until it popped off with an explosion of champagne, spewing full force at Tommy, soaking his face and upper torso. Tommy initially stood in shock, as he grabbed for something to dry his dripping face.

"Oh, you're real good at it all right!" raged Tommy.

Dennis, trying hard to stay composed, immediately intervened, and suggested, "Billy, you leave the opening to Tommy, and you and I can just start pouring." Oh, what a day this is going to be, Dennis thought. He was thankful when he heard the guests arriving.

The small horde of guests clamored in chatting and laughing as they looked for their assigned seats. Generally, everyone knew each other from either the Sahara or from Conor's, the local bar usually frequented by the Callahan's neighbors. Others, like their family members and Patricia's former bowling partners Vinny and Carol, had become acquainted during visits throughout her long recuperation. What they all had in common was a disdain for "The Gent", and a shared hope for a happy future now that Patricia and David had recommitted to one another.

Dennis was grateful when Allie, the bar server from Conor's, offered her assistance in serving the growing crowd at the bar. He was very happy to relieve the "calamity cohorts" of their bar duties, despite their disappointment.

"Would everyone please take their place?" requested the D.J.

"Thank you," he went on, after he was satisfied everyone was settled. He announced, "Now I would like you to stand and greet our guests of honor."

When the doors opened he grandly proclaimed, "Mr. and Mrs. David Callahan a-n-n-n-d Robby." The three entered to a huge roar of applause and whistling, with Robby trying to swing between them as they tightly held his hands. Nancy immediately reached for Robby and temporarily took him into her care as the happy couple faced each other.

"The song our loving couple has chosen is *Our Prayer,* sung by Celine Dion and Andrea Boccelli."

The two danced closely as they looked intently into each other's eyes and sang along:

"I pray You'll be our eyes
And watch us where we go
And help us to be wise
In times when we don't know
Let this be our prayer
When we lose our way

Lead us to a place
Guide us with Your grace
To a place where we'll be safe..."

During the song David could feel Patricia's strength waning, so he lifted her gently into his arms, finished their dance gracefully, and carried her to a seat, as the group again applauded the loving couple.

"Now can we have Jack, our best man come forth to give the toast?" the emcee blared.

Jack stood, took a deep breath, cleared his throat, lifted his champagne glass and began:

"It's been a long hard road with a few detours for Patricia and David, but they have given testimony to all of us here as to what true love is. Their love and determination has inspired many of the friendships that we now share with each other. Their compassion and forgiveness make them two very special people. I, with all of you, am very thankful to have them in my life. To a long and much smoother road ahead," he toasted, as he lifted his glass higher and looked at Patricia with tears in his eyes.

"Here, here," all shouted in unison, as they too lifted their glasses in cheer.

Patricia slowly made her way to Jack and kissed him on the cheek. "Thank you, Jack. That was a beautiful speech." She leaned towards him as if to kiss him again, and in a whisper, added, "I wish I could find a way to relieve you of your guilt."

"It was I that caused you all that suffering," he confessed. "I introduced you to that piece of garbage, and I should've shared my suspicions before he was able to hurt you so badly."

"No, Jack, I made my own choices," she emphatically stated. "He duped us all. He was a true chameleon. Please, I need you to realize that without him in my life at the time, we wouldn't have Robby. And so I thank you for that introduction. My son brings David and me such joy…he filled the void and made our lives whole. Our little miracle makes every ache and pain worth it. Please, Jack, there is nothing to forgive."

"Hey you two, mind if I interrupt?" said David, sensing the situation as he walked towards them. He had watched Jack agonizing for some time now, feeling responsible for the damaged trust Matt had left behind after he absconded without any warning. After Patricia's accident, Jack tortured himself about how he could have prevented it, if only he'd warned her about Matt. Jack's wife was really bothered by this fixation, and divorced him soon after. The timing may have been coincidental, and of course, there were probably other factors, but David was convinced that Jack's guilt had taken its toll on his already troubled marriage.

"I was just about to tell Patricia that I am moving back to New York. I miss the city. My kids are older now, and they're excited about being able to visit me there."

"What about your job?" David asked.

"I already have something waiting for me. I've always kept connections with my old foremen in New York," Jack explained.

Although she was convinced that this was a good change for Jack, Patricia felt compelled to say, "I hope when we move we won't be too far from you. We need you in our lives, Jack."

"From what I understand, Cedar Grove is not far off Route 3 which runs right into the Lincoln Tunnel. And don't you worry, I have no intention of deserting my godson," he avowed.

"Hey, what do you say if we help you move and you help us move?" David suggested with humor.

"You've got yourself a deal," Jack agreed. Robby stood next to him signaling that he wanted to be picked up by tugging repeatedly on his pant leg. "Looks like they are serving our meals," Jack said as he lifted Robby. "C'mon Bud, let's go eat." They headed towards the table.

"Perfect playmates," said David to Patricia, with his arm around her waist as they slowly made their way back.

"You made a great choice for Godfather," Patricia praised him, as she eased herself into the chair. "Jack and Robby have really bonded. What I was saying to Jack before you came over was that I am actually grateful to him for introducing me to Matt, since if he hadn't, we would never have had Robby!"

As soon as the words were out of her mouth, Patricia realized what a mistake it had been to repeat this to David. Even though it was an honest admission, it obviously pained David still to think of Patricia with Matt, and to be reminded exactly how Robby was conceived. She regretted saying this to David even more, when she saw the dark look that came into his eyes. This was not something she'd anticipated, and she was so afraid their wedding day was ruined. Patricia's fears were alleviated within a few minutes, however, when David took her hand, and gave her a soft smile. He said, "Patricia, I understand why you feel that way, but I'd rather we just concentrate on the rest of our lives now. I can't even find the words to tell you how happy I am today, and how grateful I am that we have found each other again." He kissed her then, and she knew he meant every word. David wished there was a way of eliminating Matt from the equation of their lives.

The celebration continued with live entertainment from Tommy and Billy. They tore up the floor like two dancing fools trying to impress the available girls. Fortunately for them, Alexa and Karly fell for their goofy charm, and partnered with them in hopes of improving their dance form while avoiding becoming part of the comedy act.

"All right, it's time for all the single ladies to join the bride on the dance floor please," announced the D.J.

He certainly didn't have to ask twice, as they ran barefoot toward the bride seated with her back to them. They felt restricted in their heels, and wanted to be as agile as possible in reaching for the bouquet. There was a musical drumroll, the bouquet was tossed, and a melee ensued as the women pushed and jabbed at each other for the prize. Karly and

Alexa both had their dibs on it as they each pulled apart the flower arrangement. However, Karly having secured the greater remains, including the ribbons, was proclaimed winner. The other disappointed women returned to their seats, Alexa dejectedly holding on to her small souvenir of a lost marital superstition.

David appeared on the floor waving a garter as a tease for the men. He didn't remove the garter publicly from Patricia's thigh, not wanting to expose her scarred and mangled legs. They had brought a second one, but he looked forward to removing the authentic one later in private.

"Okay guys, it's your …," he didn't even get a chance to finish before the herd of bulls darted for the floor with Tommy and Billy shoving each other out of the way in order to secure the most advantageous position. As David threw the garter back over his head, they jumped, collided and landed in a chaotic heap. Jack was at the bottom of the pile clutching the much coveted garter. When the group had finally extricated themselves from the melee, Billy and Tommy were still rolling on the floor swinging at each other for being the cause of the other's loss.

"I had it right in my hand. Why did you have to push me?" accused Tommy.

Billy continued to blame Tommy. "It was mine. *You* took it from me!"

"Well I have it now," said Jack in a teasing manner. "Looks like I still have what it takes fellas," he taunted them. Neither of the two were about to disrespect their foreman on or off the job. He was always the calming force in ending their shenanigans. The two sore losers sulked and headed toward the bar. They didn't want to watch Jack put the garter on Karly's leg, especially because they knew he would show them up again in his classy way. Dennis saw them coming and conveniently told Allie he was taking a break.

David approached Dennis saying, "I want to thank you for that profound advice you gave me a while back. Remember what you said when I was still pining for Patricia, and she wouldn't have me back? *Let it all play out regardless of how long it takes.* Those were your exact words."

"That was right here at the Sahara the night before Patricia's accident, wasn't it?" Dennis asked.

"Things could've ended so differently for me, had I not listened to you. I wanted to confront her with the info I had privately secured about that chameleon. Do you know that when Patricia woke up after the accident, she told me that the last thing she remembered about that night was the light-hearted conversation we had shared?"

"I am just so happy that you both found your way back to each other," Dennis said sincerely.

"Me too," David answered as Patricia approached them.

"May I have a quick dance, Dennis?"

"Of course," he said. "I'm honored to be asked". With that, he led her on to the dance floor.

She quickly shouted to David, "Don't go too far, my love. It's almost time to cut the cake."

"I'll be right here waiting for you!" he answered. He watched Patricia hobbling on the dance floor with Dennis, and knew he had to take her home very soon. He felt that she must be in a tremendous amount of pain by now, but realized she wouldn't say anything because she'd want to be here until the end of the party. Looking at her intently, it was still so hard to believe she had only resumed walking three weeks ago. Her stamina and determination to walk again amazed him.

"Dennis, I truly miss working with you. You were the shoulder I laughed and cried on. You were always able to make simple sense for me out of pure chaos. Please promise that you will keep in touch and also come visit us in Jersey." Patricia was on the verge of tears.

"How can I forget you after all the memorable times we shared working at the Sahara?" he responded sincerely. Then, to lighten things up, he asked, "Remember that night when some girl threw a glass of red wine in her boyfriend's face? It was like a soap opera!"

"Of course I do! That guy was a creep. Well, I guess there's more than one in this world!" Then, realizing she was bringing up Matt yet again, she changed the subject. "Oh, what about the smoking wires in the basement that set off the fire alarm. I couldn't believe the number of fire trucks that raced to the scene! Lucky for us there weren't many customers that day. It could have been so much worse trying to get everybody out. At least it didn't turn out to be anything serious."

"Hey, how come none of those things happened when I worked with any other waitress?" Dennis inquired teasingly.

"I have a magical tendency to attract excitement, I guess," she answered in good humor. They hugged each other tightly as the music stopped and their dance came to an end. He took her arm and started steering her off the dance floor.

David was waiting for her just as he said he would. "Let's say we cut the cake so that we can sneak out of here. I'm looking forward to being alone with you, Mrs. Callahan," he purred.

"I like that idea very much, Mr. Callahan," she coyly whispered.

David knew Patricia had overdone it today. He was afraid she would suffer for it over the next week or so. The sooner he got her home, the sooner he would be able to tend to her aches and pains.

The beautiful two tiered wedding cake was wheeled over to them. While the two were participating in the ritual of feeding each other a forkful, they were careful not to smear each other intentionally as they had at their first wedding. Robby, who was on the other side of the cake, was instituting his own ritual. When he reappeared from behind to see what the excitement was, his face was full of whipped cream as were his hands. He couldn't understand why everyone was laughing at him while he continued to lick the cream from his hands. Nancy quickly took him to the ladies' room to clean him up while his exhausted parents gave sincere thanks to their guests and invited them to stay, even though it was time for them to make their exit. Nancy had agreed to keep Robby for the night and they wanted to go before Robby would have a chance to notice their absence.

After David had helped Patricia out of her wedding dress, he assisted her to bed, gave her medication, and then carefully and gently massaged her legs. As she lay in his arms, she looked up at him and said, "Thank you for loving me back to life."

"You *are* my life," he said, kissing her fervently. When their lips parted, she opened her eyes and saw genuine tears in his.

KATIE PREPARES FOR THE FUTURE

Katie was exhausted after the fourth interview this week, after months of job hunting, but she remained determined to find a decent means of support for herself and her precious daughter. When she had started looking, she had no idea how tough it was these days to find something suitable. She did get a few offers during the past weeks, but not one of them paid enough or offered the benefits she needed. Ann Marie had helped her design a presentable resume, but Katie knew just how important personal interviewing skills were in securing a job. She was on her way to Montclair for the final one today, even knowing that this was a bit further than she wanted to commute every day. However, this was an ideal bookkeeping job which offered a decent salary, full medical and dental benefits, a pension plan, and tuition aid.

She sat anxiously waiting for the second interviewer, the senior partner of this financial firm. She had already met with his assistant from the Connecticut office, who was helping to establish and organize this office before returning to her position in Connecticut. Katie had found her fascinating, and the interview veered to personal topics, after they had covered the job-related issues. Kjaer was a beautiful woman from Denmark, who told Katie she'd met her husband, Mark, twenty-five years ago. He had made a brief business trip to Denmark, and apparently she'd followed him back to the U.S. They'd been together ever since. It all sounded so romantic. Katie couldn't help feeling just a bit envious of Kjaer's obvious marital bliss. That was Matt and I once, she thought.

Kjaer had also given Katie some information about her potential boss. Mr. Callahan had recently remarried, and was relocating to the neighboring town of Cedar Grove. The commuting back and forth had been taking its toll on him. It was time taken away from his family. Katie wondered what she meant by family but thought better than to inquire. Her reverie was interrupted when the door opened and a tall pleasant looking gentleman walked in.

"Hello Kathleen, I'm David Callahan, the senior partner here at Callahan and Brewer."

He extended his hand as she stood to shake it. "Thank you for waiting. We're very busy moving in and organizing offices and staff." He spoke with a professional kindness while he perused her resume as well as the notes Kjaer had made during the first interview.

"Please call me Katie. I didn't mind waiting. Kjaer told me there was a lot going on here at the moment." Katie tried not to sound as nervous as she felt.

"I'm looking for someone who is extremely responsible and on whom I can totally rely. Right now I need a personal secretary-slash-bookkeeper. Depending on how fast the firm grows, the job functions may change in the future," he explained. He looked directly at her, as though he were assessing her reaction to this statement. "I see you haven't worked recently," he stated with a skeptical look. "I'm afraid this job may be a bit overwhelming for you." Almost as an afterthought, he looked up from the resume again, and met her eyes. "What do you think?"

"Mr. Callahan, right now I would welcome the challenge," she said enthusiastically, trying not to sound desperate. Oh, but she was desperate after all, wasn't she? She continued, "I am recently separated. I have a little girl that I love so very much and that I have to provide for. Right now everything has become a new beginning for me," she continued, rambling on, "just as your company has become for you." Finally, she stopped herself, realizing she'd said too much.

David looked at her intently seeing a hurt in this woman that looked familiar to him. Yes, he had been responsible for putting that same look on Patricia's face a long time ago. For a moment he lost his train of thought while wondering whether Katie's husband had been as big a heel as he. He thought she was attractive. She had long dark hair and sparkling green eyes. Her determination and strength came across clearly despite her rather petite size.

"Thank you for sharing your personal situation, but it seems you have enough stress in your life right now. Like I said before, I need someone at my beck and call, since I'll be travelling between here and the main office in Connecticut." He was attempting to emphasize the seriousness of his expectations, so she would really understand what she was getting herself into.

"Mr. Callahan, I am willing to work as hard and as long as it takes to master this job. And I have reliable babysitters for my daughter, so I can guarantee my availability."

He began again to think about Patricia and how vulnerable she was after their separation. He remembered her determination, and how she'd started working at the Sahara to fill the aching void he had created. Meanwhile, Katie sat across the desk from him waiting to be excused. She sensed he had already decided that she wasn't experienced enough for the job. Oh, maybe he *was* right and it would require more than she was able to give, but she had no choice. Yes, she was desperate and at the moment feeling emotionally tired and defeated.

David, feeling compassionate, and also experiencing a strange connection with this helpless woman, stood up and again extended his hand to Katie, "Welcome aboard! I need someone with determination like yours," he said, smiling. "Let's give it a try and see what happens."

Katie couldn't have been more shocked. She slowly rose from her chair to accept her new job with a handshake. "Thank you so much, Mr. Callahan," she said as she fought back the tears. "I won't disappoint you."

"I'll send Kjaer back in with the necessary employment forms for you to sign," he said still smiling. "By the way, when will you be available to start?" he asked, holding his breath and hoping it would be soon.

"Um, tomorrow, I guess," Katie answered, caught off guard.

"That would be great," David said with a sigh of relief. "We'll meet in the morning to go over the preliminaries. We need to get this firm organized, and the sooner, the better." He excused himself for a moment, and as he walked down the hall, he couldn't help feeling that he had righted a wrong he had done long ago. Meanwhile, he hoped that beyond this strange feeling, he had made a positive acquisition to his firm by hiring this woman.

Katie was overwhelmed with emotion. She went through the motions of signing her employment papers, thanking Kjaer as she left. She had just gotten a job after all these months, a job she really wanted, and not one she had to settle for. "Thank you, God," she kept murmuring to herself as she drove home. She had so much to do to organize her life and Laura's. She went immediately to Ann Marie's hoping to find them back from school. She needed to share her excitement with someone, and wished it could be Matt, but of course if things were good with Matt she wouldn't have been looking for a job in the first place! She felt a sudden sense of reality returning, and her heart sank.

"Oh, Ann Marie, it's an ideal job for me. It might be rough to start, but once I get the hang of it I'll be fine. My new boss is so nice. I can't believe he actually hired me on the spot. I am so happy!" Katie grabbed Ann Marie's hands and they began whirling around the kitchen like two young schoolgirls. This really was turning into an emotional roller coaster ride for Katie.

"Katie, do you want me to keep Laura again tonight?" offered Ann Marie.

"No, I think that starting tonight, we need to begin our new lives without Matt." A dark look came over her face. It's going to be so hard tell Laura about her father..."

Just then, Laura came bounding out of Suzie's room. "Oh, mom, I missed you!" She ran to Katie and gave her big hug. "And I missed Daddy too! Where is Daddy? Is he home yet?"

To help Katie avoid answering the question, Ann Marie said "I guess you'll want to be getting Laura home now," and quickly added, "Katie, you'll drop Laura off to me on your way to work tomorrow morning and I'll take the two of them to school?"

"What work?" Laura looked confused. "Why are you going to work, Mommy, and where's my Daddy?" she asked, sensing something was drastically wrong. "I feel like I haven't seen him forever."

"We'd better be going now," said Katie, as Ann Marie gave her a sheepish look, realizing she'd just spilled the beans about the job before Katie even had a chance to talk to Laura.

Matt had called Ann Marie's inebriated a few times, but she couldn't understand his slurring words and would hang up on him. Then she would leave the phone off the hook to deter him from calling back. She didn't want the girls to experience his intoxicative phone calls. She also did not share these derelict calls with Katie. She certainly didn't need any more drama.

"It's okay," Katie mouthed to her. "We'll see you girls in the morning, alright?" She walked Laura to the door, and gave Ann Marie a quick hug.

Back at their apartment, Katie looked at Laura and said, "Why don't you put on your jammies while I make us some nice hot cocoa?"

"Okay mommy, but can I stay up 'til daddy comes home?"

"That's not possible tonight," she started to say. Then she remembered Father Seamus' advice to tell Laura the truth, so she might start to adjust to Matt's absence. "I'll explain why in a minute." Katie acted as though she was distracted, looking for mugs, and added, "Hurry and get your pajamas on so we can have our cocoa."

Laura was back in a flash dressed in her pajamas wanting to hear her mom's reason for not allowing her to stay up and wait for Matt.

"Let's cozy up on the couch, sweetie," Katie told Laura, as she placed their drinks on the coffee table. She pulled a blanket around them both as they cuddled up on the sofa. "Our chocolate is too hot to drink," she said, stalling.

"Mommy, what time is daddy coming home?" Laura asked. "He can cuddle with us too like we used to. I haven't seen him in such a long time. He's always working, even on the weekends! Or I'm at Grandma's or Ann Marie's. I miss daddy! Did he go away to work in Connecticut again? That means he broke our contract he signed!"

Laura was making it even harder and Katie felt her stomach begin to twist. She quickly said a private prayer for strength and gently began, "Laura, honey, daddy isn't living with us anymore."

Laura immediately started to cry. "Why, Mommy? Doesn't he love us anymore?"

"Baby, of course he does," she said, trying to convince her daughter and herself, knowing in a minute she was going to be crying too.

"Did I make daddy mad and want to leave us, because I woke him up that time?" she sobbed.

Katie recalled Father Seamus warning that children can internalize an alcoholic's alienation and feel responsible for causing it. She hugged her tightly as she cooed into her ear, "No, of course not, honey. Daddy is very sick right now." Laura sprang up and looked at her mother, seemingly with an odd sense of relief.

"Is he in the hospital? I want to go see him right now," she demanded. "I can make him better. I know I can," she said with certainty.

Katie spontaneously reached for her and held her tightly before she could jump off the couch. "Listen, Laura, please let me explain the story to you," she said, thinking it more a nightmare than a story. Laura lay back down on her chest expecting to hear a happily-ever-after.

"Laura, Daddy has a drinking sickness that only he can cure. When he drinks he does mean things sometimes, even though he loves us," she calmly explained.

"Well Mommy, I'll just tell him not to drink, and he won't be sick anymore," she said with the naivety of a child.

"Baby, it isn't that easy. Daddy won't listen to anyone right now because he *wants* to drink." This was even harder to explain than she had thought it would be.

"Daddy has to live somewhere else until he decides to stop drinking, Laura," Katie said in a more emphatic tone. "I don't want him to hurt you or me by accident while he's drinking," she added, hoping Laura would remember the hard shove he gave her when she tried to wake him from his drunken stupor.

"Mommy, can I call him and tell him I'm sorry for waking him up?" she asked, thinking she had a solution.

Katie was becoming exasperated as she thought about the advice to attend Al-anon meetings with Laura to help her understand and deal with her father's affliction. While she still had Laura's attention, she decided to tell her more of the "story".

"You and I have to take care of each other, in case daddy doesn't want to come back to us," she said bluntly. She saw Laura giving her an incredulous look. "That's why I got a job…to support us. Ann Marie is going to take you to and from school every day and watch you until I get home."

"Mommy," Laura said in a quivering voice, "You won't leave me too, will you? I promise I'll be a good girl." With that, she started sobbing uncontrollably.

Katie hugged her with all her might, and talking through her own tears, she promised, "Laura, I will never leave you. Not ever! Honey, I am going to work every day while you go to school, but I will be at Ann Marie's to pick you up every night, I swear." She held her even tighter and they both cried until Laura fell asleep. Katie carried her into her room. From now on she wanted to keep Laura with her every minute that she was home. She realized that neither of them had even taken a sip from their mugs. She slowly emptied the cold cocoa into the sink. She felt like it was a metaphor for her life going "down the drain". She couldn't help being furious with Matt for causing so much pain and disruption to their comfortable lives. Laura was right, in her simple child's way. He just had to stop drinking. Then everything would be alright.

NEW FRIENDS

Katie was settling into her job nicely after a couple of months, while Laura adjusted to their new daily routine. I am so blessed with my little girl. She has such a wonderful disposition, thought Katie. She knew Laura was deeply troubled about the drastic change in their lives but she *rolled with the punches*, a phrase Matt frequently used. I wonder where he is and what he is doing. As she pondered his whereabouts, she became teary eyed and wondered if he missed his two favorite girls. He was gone for almost six months now. Her thoughts were interrupted when Kjaer tapped on her office door and entered with an attractive woman.

Suddenly a small boy scooted in right past them and stood smiling at Katie.

"I Wobby. Who oo," he asked Katie, bringing a broad smile to her face.

"Now, Robby mind your manners," said the other woman, who was obviously his mother.

"I soree," he said as he climbed up on one of the chairs across the desk from Katie, sat and folded his hands in his lap.

"Sorry to bother you Katie, but I thought you might like to meet Mrs. Callahan and little Robby."

"I *big* boy," responded Robby in a huff as he folded his arms across his chest in protest.

"I can see that," Katie agreed, obviously taken in by his charm.

"He reminds me so much of my daughter when she was that age," Katie fondly told Patricia.

"Where daugh'r," Robby chimed in looking around the office expecting to see a potential companion.

"She's at school honey," Katie said totally enchanted by the little tyke.

Robby sounded a grunt and slumped back in his chair with great disappointment.

"So Robby, do you like your new house?" Katie asked.

"Yes," he answered, obviously becoming bored.

"Robby, would you like to come with me and get a cookie?"

"Yea!" he shouted, scrambling from his seat.

"I'll give you a few minutes to get acquainted," said Kjaer, as she started down the hall after Robby.

"He seems quite advanced for his age," said Katie, marveling at the child's brightness.

"Yes, he is. It's hard to believe that he was born prematurely. Unfortunately that is why David and I tend to dote on him, making it hard to discipline him at times. It's so difficult for me to physically keep up with him sometimes."

"My husband and I had the same problem with our daughter. She wasn't born prematurely, but she has engaged us into negotiations sometimes as though she were an adult," Katie said, smiling in adoration of Laura. "We never even realize until it's too late."

"I hope you don't mind me asking," Patricia said in genuine concern, "but has anything changed with your situation at home? David told me you've had your share of trials lately."

"No, we're still separated. He hasn't stopped drinking, and he doesn't seem to want to stop anytime soon," she sighed. She was dismayed and a little surprised at her own words and the fact that she was sharing so much with this woman she had just met.

"I am so sorry to hear that. I remember the pain of our separation and later divorce. It was one of the hardest times of our lives, but we managed to pull it together again and now we couldn't be happier." Patricia offered this brief summation in earnest. "If there is anything at all that I can do for you, please don't hesitate to call on me."

"Thank you. That is so nice of you,"

"Oh well, I guess I should go save Kjaer from my beguiling tot."

Patricia winced in pain when trying to stand. "Are you okay?" Katie asked, as she rose from her desk to help.

"No, I can do it. I am still recuperating from an accident I had a while ago."

"Oh dear, what happened?" she asked. She watched as Patricia reached for her cane which Katie hadn't noticed when they walked in earlier.

"It's a long story but one I want to forget," she said politely. She quickly changed the subject by saying, "We're having a house-warming party in the next month or so. Would you like to come?"

"That would be wonderful, but I usually spend all my free time with my daughter since I started working," Katie answered with some disappointment.

"Why don't you bring her? That is, of course, if she doesn't mind a pesky toddler."

"I am sure she would love him. She has all the patience in the world for children younger than herself. She transforms into a little mother."

"Great, then, I'll be sending invitations in the near future. We want to be settled and comfortable in our new home first."

"If you need any help, I would be glad to jump in," Katie freely offered.

"Thank you. I may need some," she said as she leaned on her cane to walk. "It was so nice to meet you. I can see David made a wise decision when he hired you. I think that you are truly a great asset to him."

"Thank you. I am so grateful for the opportunity he gave me. You are both so kind."

"Well, you have certainly proved yourself worthy of our praise. You've exceeded David's expectations. Kjaer will be glad to go back to work in the Connecticut office next week."

"I'll miss her terribly," Katie admitted.

"We will too. I try to remind myself that she is only a phone call away. She has become family to us. I'm sure you both will be communicating frequently about business. From what David tells me the offices will be very interactive."

"I hope so."

Their female bonding was suddenly interrupted by the sound of a toddler's fast moving feet heading in their direction.

"I 'elp." Robby said as he took Patricia's free hand by his little one and led her down the hall. While the two wobbled along to say their good-byes to David, Katie's eyes filled up with tears at the sight. The child had the compassion of a saint.

Katie was excited to hear that the Callahans were happy with her work. She clasped her hands in sheer glee. It gave her great satisfaction to know she was accomplishing something in her life despite her personal turmoil. She immediately felt a warm kinship toward Patricia and sensed that they had a lot in common. But she was also intrigued by Patricia's statement, "but we managed to pull it together again and now we couldn't be happier." There must be a story there. Kjaer had also inadvertently made dubious comments about the personal lives of the Callahans which Katie didn't want to question so as not to appear nosey. And there was the accident that she obviously didn't want to talk about. Regardless, God had sent these wonderful people into her life at a much needed time, and she would always be grateful to them.

Katie was again engrossed in her work when she was interrupted this time by the ringing of her cell phone.

"Hello?" she answered, not recognizing the number on the caller ID.

"Yes, this is Mrs. Reilly." There was a pause. The person on the other end asked her some questions about Matt. Then they told her what had happened. "Oh, my God! Where is he?" She reached for her coat and started down the hall.

David and Kjaer were discussing the progress of the new office when they heard Katie frantically exclaim "I'll be right there!" She barged in, with one arm in a coat sleeve, trying to shift the phone to put on the other. She looked at them and said, "I'm so sorry but I have an emergency. My husband is in the hospital. He fell and hit his head."

"Do you want me to take you to him?" David asked deeply concerned. "I don't think that you should be driving right now."

Katie paused and took a deep breath, "No thank you, I'll be okay. It's just a shock. The hospital said he would be okay but he is asking for me."

"Please be careful," Kjaer said, giving her a quick hug.

"Call us and give us an update when you can. And whatever you do, don't worry about your work. We can take care of it," David shouted after her, speaking for himself and Kjaer.

Katie hurried down the hall of the hospital and was relieved when she found Ann Marie standing outside of Matt's room. She was talking to a man she didn't recognize.

"I'm so glad you're here Ann Marie," Katie said. They hugged. "Have you seen him yet? How is he?"

"We don't know yet. I just got here. I ran out of the house when you called. The doctor is in with him now. This is Kevin, Matt's friend from work. He was with Matt when he got hurt."

The fella stepped forward extending his hand to shake hers, and Katie shook it with caution.

"Hello, Kevin. We finally get to meet. Matt has told me a lot of about you. He refers to you as St. Kevin."

"Oh, I don't know about that. I wasn't able to prevent this from happening."

"What did happen?"

Before he could answer, the doctor approached the group and asked to speak to Mrs. Reilly.

"I'm she," Katie said quickly as she anxiously stepped toward him.

"Mrs. Reilly, I'm Dr. Fallon."

"How is he? Is he all right?"

"Well, maybe we should talk over there," he said nodding to a more private area.

"Excuse us, please," she said to Ann Marie and Kevin, and followed the doctor across the hall.

"Mrs. Reilly, your husband has a major concussion from hard forced trauma to his head that he should recover from. It's the alcoholism that concerns me. How long has he been drinking this heavily?"

"Doctor, I don't know the real answer. About six months ago, he came home from a business trip. He was drunk that night and as far as I know, he hasn't stopped. I threw him out soon after. I have no idea where he's been since. He's become a total stranger to me."

The doctor fixed Katie with a serious stare. "If he continues to keep drinking at this pace, he'll be dead within a few years, maybe less. Let's see if we can keep him here a couple of days, so that he can detox. Then we can go from there. If I let him out now in this condition he's in, he'll go right back to the bar. I would strongly suggest AA, and possibly some sort of therapy. Maybe he needs to talk to someone. We'll try to arrange that while he's here."

"Thank you, Doctor. I totally agree with everything you've just told me. Can I see him now?"

"Yes, but keep it short. The longer he sleeps it off, the more receptive to help he may be."

"Thank you so much, Doctor."

"You're very welcome, Mrs. Reilly."

Katie turned to Ann Marie and Kevin. "I'm only going in for a few minutes. Kevin, would you mind waiting with Ann Marie? I really would like to talk to you some more about Matt."

"Sure," he answered. Katie sensed from his hasty response that he welcomed the opportunity to be alone with Ann Marie.

"Why don't we go to my house to talk?" offered Ann Marie. "The girls will be home from school soon, and I want to be there when they get off the bus."

"I don't mind," agreed Kevin.

"Great. I'll meet you both there as soon as I can," Katie said and walked into Matt's dimly lit room with some trepidation.

Katie watched Matt while he slept restlessly. He suddenly jerked and began mumbling. She tried to listen intently but could only make out a few words. She thought it sounded like he was saying sorry, wish…wait, was that 'trish'? His speech was so garbled. She heard her name…'Katie, Katie'. She was pathetically happy to know that he was still thinking about her. She wanted so much to kiss him, but was afraid of waking him up. She sat patiently next to his bed and held his hand. If only I knew what was torturing you, maybe I could help, she thought.

Katie did not realize that she was witnessing Matt suffering from alcohol withdrawal, despite the medication he was given to ease the transition. He was experiencing delirium tremens accompanied with frightful hallucinations. He continued to thrash and mumble.

> *There were two people standing at his bedside, one on the left and one on the right. He tried to focus harder to see who they were. It was then that he assumed that he was on his deathbed. Better yet, he was praying that he was. He closed his eyes tight and then quickly opened them again only to find the two women still standing there glaring at him. He had been hoping that they were part of his sickly delirium. He recognized then that it was Katie and Patricia. Both women began leaning in, closing in on him, as they shouted in unison, "I HATE YOU! I HATE YOU!" Their chanting became louder and more vindictive. Frantically, he tried hurling his body forward to try and get past the both of them, only to find that he had jumped out of the bed head first…*

Katie watched as he seemed to become more agitated and suddenly bolted upright. He was sweating profusely and panting heavily.

"Matt, it's Katie," she said softly. She didn't want to say too much. He smelled like old stale liquor. He looked unkempt and very thin.

"Katie, I am so glad you're here," he said, clearly relieved to see her as he lay back on his pillow. "My head hurts."

"The doctor said that you have a bad concussion from a fall." She was hoping that he would elaborate on the details. Instead he closed his eyes, and asked, "When can I get out of here?"

"I don't know. The doctor said they would keep you a couple of days for observation." She didn't want to mention detoxing to him. She felt that he would listen better, if it came from his doctor.

"Is Laura with you? I miss you and my little princess so mu-much. I want to come ho-home," he said weakly, as he nodded back off to sleep hoping not to meet the two angry women again in his dreams.

Katie gave him a gentle kiss on his forehead before leaving. She had missed him too. She desperately wanted their happily-ever-after lives back. She decided not to tell Laura that Matt was in the hospital. She thought it better to wait a couple of days to see if Matt would commit to stop drinking.

Katie smiled when she found Kevin and Ann Marie sitting in the kitchen chatting like old friends, although they had only met at the hospital. They were sharing their intimate stories of lost love since they were both "victims" – Kevin having been stood up at the altar, and Ann Marie having been betrayed by Rory. Kevin was the first to notice Katie's presence.

"How is Matt?"

"The doctor says he'll be fine if he stops drinking. Matt said that he wants to come back home, but he fell back asleep before we could discuss anything. I don't want to say anything to Laura until we know for sure."

"That's probably a good idea," agreed Ann Marie.

"Where are the girls?" Katie asked. "It's very quiet in here."

"They're watching Cinderella in Suzie's bedroom."

"I don't want to interrupt their prince charming fantasy," she said as she sat down to join them for tea.

"Kevin, how did Matt fall?" Katie asked as she poured herself a cup.

"He was defending a girl from some abusive jerk who was annoying her, while she was sitting talking with us."

"The knight in shining armor rides again," Katie cheered facetiously.

"Not quite," said Kevin. "He fell off his horse when the guy punched him in the face so hard, that he fell backwards and was knocked out."

"Why was the guy upset that the girl was talking to you?" Ann Marie joined in.

"She's a bar floozy. I personally can't stand this girl, Nikki, but every time we walk in, she makes her way over and manages to strike up a conversation with Matt." He related this in a detached manner, not meaning to betray his absent buddy.

"What bar is this?" Ann Marie asked.

"The Irish Pub. It's near the YMCA. It's a great place."

"Really," Katie responded caustically.

Realizing that he may have sounded a bit too insensitive to the present matter at hand, he stuttered, "I-I- like to chat with the barman there. You call him Kieran." He quickly added, "We were both born in the same district in Belfast."

"Do you and Matt go there every day?" Ann Marie asked, trying not to appear obvious in her personal interest in him.

"I've been going with Matt a couple of times a week after work. I met him there earlier today for a quick lunch. He said he's on a mission to get me out more to socialize." Kevin purposely mentioned this for Ann Marie's behalf. "I get the feeling that he doesn't like being alone. Besides, I want to be sure that he doesn't get into trouble, and that no one takes advantage of him." Kevin was referring to Nikki and her aggressive behavior toward Matt, but didn't verbalize those details.

"Thank you," said Katie, truly appreciating his concern. "I only wish I knew what happened in Connecticut to start all this. He's been drinking since he's returned," she said as she looked toward Kevin for some kind of an answer.

"I really don't know," he honestly replied. "I was very surprised that he didn't stay with his foreman, Jack, like he did the first time. It's strange because Jack could have chosen Matt to work for him again. They seemed so tight. I know he was extremely disappointed that he didn't see or work with the same crew as before."

"I know. Jack even lent him his car to come home on two occasions," Katie added in agreement.

"I guess you'll never know unless he shares the story with you, Katie," Ann Marie chimed in.

"You're right. He said he wants to come home and that he is tired of drinking. I pray that he really means it. I don't want to tell Laura in case he changes his mind. She has had her share of disappointments lately."

"Kids are resilient," said Ann Marie.

Katie quickly responded, "Sometimes the scars aren't exposed until later in life, and that is my concern. I want to protect my little girl from any more needless heartache."

"What a great mom you are," Kevin said with genuine respect.

"Thank you. I try," she replied "I'll have to clean out the liquor cabinet before Matt comes home. That's a priority. AA suggests keeping a liquor-free home. Maybe either of you would want it? Kevin, why don't you bring Ann Marie by my house sometime in the next couple of days to pick it up?" she suggested, sensing that there was a strong attraction between the two.

Kevin was quick to answer, "Sure." He looked at Ann Marie for her approval, confirming Katie's suspicions. She inadvertently smiled at the thought that Matt had once previously suggested matching the two up on a blind date. He unintentionally managed to do that with his drunken escapade.

The next couple of days were hectic for Katie. She was leaving work early, going to the hospital to see Matt, and then picking up Laura a bit later than usual, citing that she was detained at work.

She called Father Seamus to give him an update on Matt's situation since she had last seen him at Sunday Mass. She trusted the humble priest's advice and spiritual guidance. She knew the "young man Matt" that the congregation prayed for the last few Sundays was her Matt, and she was grateful for the much needed prayers.

He was happy to hear that Matt's fall wasn't serious, and that he was willing to stop drinking. "There are a couple of things that I would like you to remember Katie. Matt is emotionally weak at the moment, but as he becomes stronger so may his attitude. He may be remorseful now, but once the little demons in his brain tell him he can handle drinking, the roller coaster ride begins again. Matt may think he's cured and that he can handle a drink or two, but if he starts to drink he will start at the same pace as when he stopped. We alcoholics in our early stages tend to indulge in a lot of false hopes, because we don't want to believe we have a weakness. As much as you may want to believe him, don't fall for it. Because realistically, I will tell you that many times alcoholics fall off the wagon before they accept their disease."

"Oh Father, he knows I won't allow him to drink anymore," Katie said emphatically.

"I'm sorry to tell you, but you have nothing to do with it. He has to want to not drink. He has to understand the consequences for himself. Katie, I don't want to burst your bubble, but I want you to be aware of the possibilities ahead. I will continue to pray for Matt and yourself, dear, and I hope Matt will join you and Laura at weekly Mass."

"Hopefully he will want to come along with us this week. Thank you for taking time to talk to me. Goodbye, Father."

"You are very welcome. You know you may call me at any time, Katie. God bless you," he said as he hung up.

Katie pondered what the priest had said, but she was determined to stay optimistic and keep Matt sober at any cost.

Katie had agreed that Matt could return home as long as he didn't drink, promised to attend AA meetings regularly and sought therapy. He refused the therapy, but reluctantly agreed to go to AA.

"I really don't have a drinking problem. I was just having a mid-life crisis," Matt tried to convince her, but she remembered the priest's prediction that Matt might say something like this.

"Matt, you know the agreement about your returning home. I don't ever again want Laura or myself to experience your abusive drunken behavior!" Katie stated quite adamantly.

"Okay, okay," he agreed.

She made a list of the different meetings in their area so that Matt would be able to schedule them. She offered to go with him to the open meetings. She understood that the closed ones were only for the recovering alcoholics because of the personal stories they shared. Katie was willing to make any necessary adjustments to her life in order to keep her family together.

Laura and Suzie were watching TV in the living room, when the Reillys' front door opened and Matt walked in ahead of Katie.

"Daddy, Daddy you're home!" Laura cried as she ran toward him with open arms. He snatched her up, and they both hugged as Laura cried, "Oh, Daddy I missed you so much. I won't ever try to wake you up again."

Katie made Matt aware of his earlier drunken antics. She didn't want to make him feel guilty, but wanted him to be aware of the effects his drinking had on herself and Laura.

"Laura, it wasn't your fault honey. I drank too much but you won't have to worry about that anymore. I'm so sorry, baby," he said as he clutched her tighter. "I love you and mommy so much."

"Hi Matt," Ann Marie called from the kitchen. "Welcome home," she added as she entered the room to give him a hug. She had prepared dinner for the Reilly family. She knew Katie was overwhelmed with reorganizing their lives.

"Thanks Ann Marie," he said. "I'm so sorry for my behavior toward you," he said sheepishly, still holding Laura.

"I'm just so happy that we have our old Matt back," Ann Marie replied as she reached around Laura to kiss his cheek.

Laura had her arms tightly wrapped around his neck, so as to never let him go.

"Mommy, did you tell Matt about your new boyfriend?" Suzie announced with her own excitement.

Matt smiled at Ann Marie while she blushed like a smitten teenager. Katie had already filled him in about the budding romance between Ann Marie and Kevin. He couldn't have been more pleased. After all, it was originally his idea to match the two up.

"That's the best news I've heard in a long time," he said as he winked at Ann Marie. "Do you like Kevin?" Matt asked Suzie.

"Oh yes, he's so nice and he makes my Mommy so happy."

"We'd better get home if we want to see the 'nice' man," Ann Marie said.

"Why don't you have him come here, so we can all enjoy the night together?" Matt offered.

"Thanks Matt but another time. You three need your own time together."

Suzie managed to eke out, "I'm so glad you're home too." She quickly hugged Matt's leg before they left.

Katie was very relieved that Ann Marie had the sense to realize that their family needed their private time to heal and recover from their ordeal. Besides she thought she noticed Matt shaking slightly every once in a while. The doctor explained this was to be expected as a withdrawal symptom, but that it should subside with time. A quiet family night was definitely in order for them.

"Daddy, Mattie missed you too," Laura said. "He hasn't been the same since you left, but I know he'll be better now that you're home," she said taking Matt's hand to lead him into her bedroom to see her beloved chameleon.

"Mattie, look who's home. Now you can feel better," she softly said as she cautiously reached into the tank to take him out. The creature retreated into his corner. Laura was disappointed that Mattie didn't respond to Matt's return as she had expected. Maybe he too was upset that Matt stayed away so long, she thought to herself.

"Hey, you two, dinner is on the table," Katie called in a cheerful tone, trying to make it seem like things were back to normal.

Laura followed Matt around like a puppy for the rest of the night, and he indulged her with hugs and kisses to reassure her that he wasn't going to leave her again. After she finally fell asleep in his lap, Matt carried her to her room, and gingerly placed her in bed so as not to wake her up.

"I didn't think our little chaperone was ever going to leave us alone," Matt quipped as he pulled Katie into his arms on the couch.

"I think that she's afraid you may leave if she takes her eyes off you for a second," Katie explained.

"I'm not going anywhere," he said as he began to kiss her neck.

"You'd better not," she murmured, responding to his advances. She had missed his sexual adeptness.

The two began desperately removing each other's clothes as their breathing progressed into rhythmic panting but their romantic interlude came to an abrupt stop as Matt collapsed on top of her.

"What's wrong?"

"I don't know. It just deflated. I'm so sorry," he whispered in embarrassment and frustration while he hid his head in her sprawling hair.

"Matt, it's okay. It's only the temporary effect of the medication you're taking," she said softly, trying to soothe his bruised ego. Katie was well aware that Matt was very proud of his sexual prowess. She lifted his head up so she could look into his eyes to reassure him, "Matt, we have the rest of our lives together." She kissed him passionately, and then allowed him to rest his weary head on her chest. She calmed him and finally, he fell asleep.

BACK ON THE ROLLERCOASTER

The next few weeks were an adjustment for the Reilly family. Matt had become moody and wasn't always his optimistic, playful self. He became anxious without any provocation. Katie worried about him while she worked, but soon came to the realization that his sobriety was up to him. He knew what the stakes were if he gambled with a drink. Katie had to coax him into attending his meetings on a regular basis. After attending a few, he announced that he didn't need them anymore because he was back to normal. He wasn't like those other people; he didn't lose his job or his family and friends. He temporarily lost sight of the important things. He would make suggestions of things to do in place of going to the meetings. He wanted them to rejoin their bowling league, but Katie advised him that they were already replaced at her own suggestion. She didn't think it was a good idea for Matt to be around liquor for the time being. Matt's sponsor, Jim, agreed it was too soon, since their previous bowling nights had been centered on social drinking. He recommended that Matt not put himself in a position or place of temptation until he got emotionally stronger. His attitude got better when he returned to work full-time but eventually suggested that Katie quit hers.

"You don't need to work anymore, Katie. You should be home taking care of our house and Laura," he insisted.

"Matt, I love my job and my boss and I have no intention of leaving them," she adamantly responded.

"What about Laura? She needs you home with her after school," he continued trying to prompt a guilt trip.

"Laura is just fine with Suzie and Ann Marie after school. Don't worry. I arranged my hours so that I will be home when you get out of work," she said, well-aware of his attempt to emotionally manipulate her.

"Umph," he grunted in defeat. This would be a matter to debate at a later time. "So what's with this boss of yours? Do I have any reason to be jealous of him?" he asked trying to sound playful.

"Who, David? He's such a great guy," Katie paused, trying to tease him. She then added, "He is very happily married to a wonderful woman, Patricia. I call her Trish." Katie thought she may have seen a wince from Matt. She hoped he wasn't starting the shakes again but continued, "We have already become fast friends. In fact, I feel like she is my idol," Katie averred.

"Why's that?"

"That poor woman has been through so much. She was in a bad car accident a while ago and never thought she'd walk again. I sense the pain she is in with every step she takes. She has a little toddler, Robby, who keeps her very busy, and yet he is very sensitive toward her debilitation and tries to help her. He is like a little old man. He reminds me of our little old lady," she added chuckling.

"Wow, that's too bad. She must have her hands full if he's anything like Laura. She'd better start taking Law 101 to learn negotiation skills."

"I told her the same. By the way, they're having a house-warming party in a couple of weeks and we're invited. You can meet them then; I think Laura will enjoy their little boy."

"Sounds great! That's something to look forward to, but what's on for tonight?" Matt asked eagerly.

"Ann Marie and Kevin asked if we were interested in taking the girls out for ice cream tonight. We'll wait for you after your meeting and we can all walk to Carvel."

"Why don't I skip the meeting tonight and we can go earlier?" Matt suggested, hoping Katie would agree.

"No, they have things to do before," she lied trying to keep him focused. "Is tonight's meeting open or closed?"

"Open, why?"

"I'd love to go with you. We can drop Laura at Ann Marie's on the way." Katie was committed to supporting Matt in staying sober. She was sensing Matt's waning disinterest in AA. She felt awkward at the meetings, but understood the recovering alcoholics needed AA as a means of survival. Only they could truly understand and share the struggles of their addiction. She wasn't sure if Matt had bought into the philosophy and doctrine of AA, but she constantly encouraged him to read the *Big Book*, AA's "bible of sobriety" by reading and sharing it with him. She intended it to be his new way of life.

"Are you sure you want to come?" he asked her.

"Yes, very much so," she answered as she gently kissed his lips.

"Well, maybe we could skip the meeting," he said as he pulled her toward him.

"Never mind," she said as she pulled away. "We have a very important date tonight." She hurried out of the room before she could fall prey to his suggestion.

Katie and Matt were greeted by a friendly group as they walked into the AA meeting held in the basement of the local Episcopal Church. Matt's sponsor, Jim, was glad to see them there together. Katie took the opportunity to talk to him when Matt went to the men's room.

"Jim, I sense a bit of unrest with Matt, and am not sure how I should handle it. He doesn't think he needs these meetings anymore. He is convinced that he isn't an alcoholic. I am so confused. Maybe he's right. Maybe he was just having a mid-life crisis. How can we tell?" she asked in desperation.

"Give him a drink and you'll know soon enough!"

"Why would I do that!" she snapped.

"Katie, once the alcohol hits his blood you'll know, because he won't be able to stop. From what he has shared with me, which isn't much, but given his daily sudden pattern of drinking, I am sure he is an alcoholic. He couldn't stop drinking on his own. It took an accident to stop him. Isn't that right?"

"You're right," she agreed as Matt came back on the scene.

"Looks like the meeting is starting. Let's grab a seat," prompted Jim.

The room quieted as the main speaker of the night was introduced. The night's speaker was Jim unbeknownst to neither Katie nor Matt. He took the stage and proudly announced, "Hello, I'm Jim and I'm an alcoholic." The room resounded with affirmation, "Hi Jim." He began his story with the successes of his earlier life. He had married a beautiful accomplished woman, bought a massive home in a well groomed neighborhood, had two wonderful children, and possessed a job worthy of every man's envy. Life was good to him. That is until his casual drinking became binging, and then escalated to a daily obsession. He stopped drinking a couple of times, trying to convince himself he could control his drinking, but he would only start up as badly as when he left off. His drinking career came to an abrupt halt one rainy night when he picked up his beloved son and his friend from football practice. He had been drinking all day and was sloshed, as he put it. He couldn't remember anything else about the night, but was later told that he drove off the road and hit a telephone pole at seventy miles an hour. His son and the friend were killed instantly, since he had irresponsibly let them sit together in the front seat with no seatbelts. Jim began softly crying, as he continued with the rest of his story. There wasn't a dry eye in the room as he related that not only did he lose his son, but also his life as he had known it. His wife refused to talk to him from that night on, except through her lawyer. He lost his house, his job, his money, but most of all he lost his family. After spending five years in jail, he was released back into a cold, unwelcoming world. The only solace and warmth he found was at AA with his understanding fellow alcoholics. It was fifteen years ago to the day that Jim had taken his last drink. He began his life again slowly determined to keep a humble eye on his higher power. He thanked his empathetic audience and made his way back to Katie and Matt who sat in shock after his personal disclosure. They too hugged him upon his return, as everyone else had who was in his path.

"Wow," Matt said emotionally overwhelmed, and not knowing what to say to Jim.

Katie sniveled into Jim's ear whispering, "Thank you for sharing, I hope he heard you." She and Matt soon left. They walked slowly to Ann Marie's both engrossed in their own thoughts. "The effects of alcohol are detrimental to so many people's lives," Katie murmured.

"Who would want to drink after hearing that story?" said Matt apparently affected by Jim's anniversary talk.

Thank you Jim, Katie said to herself.

Their dark cloud lifted as soon as Katie and Matt stepped into the lively living-room at Ann Marie's. The four were watching the ending of an I Love Lucy episode laughing hysterically at the sitcom antics. "I can see we're just in time for some much needed fun," Matt called over the laughter.

"Daddy, Lucy is so funny," Laura giggled as she ran to him and linked her arms around his waist.

"What did she do this time?" he asked.

"She and this lady were stomping grapes with their feet and they started fighting. They were throwing grapes at each other," she narrated.

"Yeah, and they were wrestling each other in the grapes. They were covered in grape juice," Suzie chimed in.

"Lucy is so silly isn't she?" Matt said.

"She sure is," Kevin responded. "I can watch her shows over and over and still kill myself laughing."

"Is everyone ready to go for ice cream?" Katie interrupted.

"Yes," they all screamed in unison.

The lighthearted Lucy-lovers strolled to Carvel for their ice cream and enjoyed it while they sat on benches along the Hudson waterfront. The spectacular view of the New York skyline was entertainment in itself but was enhanced by the hustle and bustle of the variety of vessels on the waterway. Suzie and Laura were standing at the rail waving to the passengers on the ferryboat leaving the New Jersey pier crossing the Hudson River to the New York side. They were amazed at a tiny tug boat pulling a ginormous ocean liner down the Hudson River through the New York Harbor. It was a pleasant peaceful night enjoyed by them all.

Matt was very happy about Kevin and Ann Marie being together. He liked having a male companion around. It was like old times before Ann Marie and Rory had divorced. The adults planned to ask Ann Marie's mom to watch the girls the following night, so the adults could double-date with dinner and a movie. In fact the next couple of weeks were busy for the two families. The girls joined a mother-daughter ceramic group. Matt continued attending his meetings and Kevin was on the scene whenever possible to join in the activities.

Katie had been excited about Matt meeting the Callahans at their house-warming party, but was disappointed when his sponsor called and recommended that Matt replace the party with an AA meeting. Jim told Katie that he believed Matt was starting to obsess about alcohol. He was talking about missing the clinking sound of ice cubes in his vodka glass. Since there may be a lot of "clinking" at the party, they agreed it would be safer for Matt to miss it, even though he was looking forward to meeting the new people in Katie's life. Matt suggested that Katie ask the Callahans to dinner at their home in the near future.

Matt was sitting on the couch watching the end of an exciting movie, and nervously twisting his hands together as Katie and Laura were ready to leave. "Daddy, maybe I should stay home with you," offered Laura.

"No honey, I'm all right. I'm going to a meeting with Jim and out for coffee after. You'll probably get home before me so don't worry. I'm okay," he said as he opened his arms to her, prompting a hug.

"Okay Daddy," she said as she ran into his arms. "Now you call us if you need us to come home," she added.

"I surely will," he agreed as he hugged her tighter.

"It's my turn now," said Katie, patiently waiting for her hug from Matt. "I thought I was the wife here," she whispered into his ear and they both smiled.

Once outside the door, Laura paused for a minute. "Mommy, I feel terrible about leaving daddy. Maybe I should stay and take care of him."

"Sweetie, daddy is going out, and you can't stay alone."

"All right then, but can I call him later?"

"Of course, but come on. I told Trish I would come early to help her get ready," she insisted, reaching for Laura's hand.

After they left, and the movie ended, Matt decided he had time for a quick jog around the neighborhood before

Jim picked him up for the meeting. He was told the exercise was good for him, both physically and mentally. When he was out running, he really didn't have time to think about how much he missed the drink. He was tired after he'd run about a mile, and decided to take a seat on the front steps of a nearby apartment building before continuing home to wait for Jim.

Matt was enjoying people watching from the stoop. A young couple walked by with their busy little boy who was stopping to talk to everyone he encountered. He stopped at the bottom of the stairs from where Matt was sitting, looked up and waved his small hand, then waddled on his way. I had always wanted a son like that, he thought. Someone I could play sports with while Katie and Laura shopped. But now was not the time to think about that, maybe when his life settled. He savored the thought that Katie would have to stop working to take care of a new baby. He looked at the dog park across the street where people walked their dogs and socialized with other dog owners. Laura loved when he took her there to sit and watch the different breeds and sizes of dogs interact. For hours after, Laura would haunt him about getting a dog. He planned on surprising her someday, when they had a house of their own in Hoboken.

Yes, Hoboken was the place to live, Matt mused. A place where one could be among people, and yet be alone if you wanted. The waterfront was only two blocks away from their apartment and the main avenue with all the shops and restaurants was only one street away in the other direction. There were always cultural fairs and events sponsored by different groups. There was always something to do here in Hoboken. And he liked that people in Hoboken were very friendly. This was his hometown and he loved it. His thoughts were interrupted by a couple walking up the stairs. Matt smiled at them and said hello, but as they got closer to him they abruptly stopped in their tracks.

"You scumbag, how dare you say hello to us after what you did to our Patricia!" the woman screamed accusingly at him. The man with her shouted too, "You son of a bitch! You turned out to be some sleaze bucket, lying to all of us. I ought to…" The woman over-shouted him, "I hope you don't live in this building. I don't want my daughter living anywhere near a despicable creature like you! And we thought you were a gentleman!" Matt was by now in total shock shaking, and not sure how to respond. "I… I… I… was out for a run and just sat here a sec. I …I… live across town," he stammered as he backed away from them down the stairs. He turned and began to run in random directions. When he stopped, he found himself pacing in front of the Irish Pub. His mind was in riddles. He suddenly remembered that they were the couple he sat next to at a dinner party with Patricia and her friends in Connecticut. In fact they were telling everyone there about a dad orchestrating a parade for his young daughter and her friends in the park across from their daughter's apartment in Hoboken. He was that dad. He had feigned a headache and left the party to avoid their questions about where he lived, since Patricia had already told them that *he* was also from Hoboken. He remembered wondering if it were possible that their daughter had lived in his building, when they were relating her story. What if he ran into them again? This nightmare is never going to end; things had been going so well for him lately. Maybe he could talk Katie into moving. That was very unlikely. She loved where they lived as much as he did. Oh, what if they see Katie and me together, he fretted. What would they do? Would they approach her and blurt out his indiscretions? He had himself in such a state that he was sweating and shaking while wringing his hands nervously together. He looked once more at the Irish Pub before opening the door and going in.

"Well what about ye?" Kieran asked him. "The usual," Matt answered obviously focused on a drink, and not on what the barman asked.

"Are you sure?" Kieran asked, knowing from Kevin that Matt was on the wagon after his drunken episode a bit back.

"Yes," Matt snapped gritting his teeth.

When the drink was in front of him, Matt hesitated for a second before lifting the glass and gulping it down. He never expected the effect of extreme nausea and he ran for the men's room and got sick. He wet his face, cleaned himself up and headed back to the bar. Kieran was not surprised. He had witnessed this same scene time and again when alcoholics would take their first drink after abstaining for a while.

"I'll have another, please," he said, feeling obviously more at ease.

Matt sipped his second drink a bit more discreetly, as he settled on his barstool for the night. It wasn't long before Nicole entered the bar wearing an extremely tight black mini skirt and a provocative low cut periwinkle blouse. She was delighted when she saw Matt, and took a seat next to him and began working her wiles. Kieran prayed Matt would be able to keep his wits about him, but was dismayed when he watched them move to a more secluded part of the bar.

Patricia welcomed Katie's help with her party. Kjaer had also come early. It gave the three ladies time to catch up. "Katie, I am so sorry your husband isn't here. I really would like to have met him," said Kjaer.

"Me too," agreed Patricia. "I've heard so much about him."

"I wanted him to meet everyone also, but his meetings are so important right now. He did tell me to arrange a dinner at our house whenever you can make it. We'll have to make a date. Kjaer, you and Mark are invited also."

"That would be so nice, we can talk later," Patricia said.

"Oh, and your daughter is an adorable little girl," Kjaer averred.

"She is everything you said she'd be," Patricia added. "She just took Robby right under her wing and now he's hooked. He's been following her around like a little puppy dog."

"They are getting along marvelously, aren't they?" Katie agreed. "There goes the doorbell," she announced, as it sounded throughout the house.

The three women went to see who the first guests were. David was just opening the door to a man and two women who must have come together. "Hey, Patricia, look who's here," David shouted, not realizing that she had just entered the room and was right behind him.

"Oh, I am so glad you could make it. Jack, thanks for bringing Marilyn and Maggie. I know how they hate long drives," she said as she hugged each one.

"Robby, someone is here to see you," David called up the stairs. Suddenly there were little footsteps heard on the floorboards above them making their way down the hall.

"Unca Jack," Robbie shouted as he tried to make his way to him.

Jack scooped him up and held him over his head as he squealed away. When Robby was put down, he took Laura by the hand and pulled her toward Jack. "Zee girfrend."

"Really? Aren't you starting a little young, son?" Jack said for the benefit of the adults who broke into giggles.

"Uh?" Robby responded with innocence causing everyone to laugh. The receiving line now extended through the living room as the rest of the guests arrived. Patricia was trying to acknowledge her guests as they arrived, and introduce them to Katie at the same time since she was the only person present who was not acquainted with the rest. It became an overwhelming feat during all the excitement, so she waited until the majority of guests were present and made a general announcement, "I'd like you all to meet David's new assistant and our new dear friend, Katie."

They all answered, "Hi Katie," in unison. It reminded Katie of the enthusiastic response to every speaker at an AA meeting. The thought caused her to wonder how Matt was doing at that moment. Everyone began to mingle and share each other's latest news. Most of them hadn't seen each other since Patricia and David's wedding. Katie was passing a small clique of women who comfortably drew her into their conversation. "Katie, my name is Marilyn, this is my sister Maggie, that is Carol, and Nancy," she continued as she pointed to each person.

"Hello ladies," Katie answered as she looked from one to another. "Did you know David and Patricia for long?"

Nancy was the first to answer, "Patricia and I met in high school and have remained close friends ever since."

Maggie offered, "Marilyn and I were regular lunch customers at the restaurant where Patricia worked."

"And Vinny and I were on Patricia's bowling league for years," added Carol. "But we all met and became close friends while taking care of Patricia after her accident. We all covered different shifts and met when we relieved each other. "The crew over there," she said as she pointed to a group of men and women sitting together talking, "are from her neighborhood. There are others who couldn't make it tonight."

"How did it happen?" asked Katie.

The women all looked around nervously. Nancy explained very quietly, "She went out in a dangerous storm to search for her boyfriend when he never came home. She thought he was stuck or hurt somewhere but the truth is he left her without saying goodbye. He was going home to a wife she never knew he had. She skidded off the road." At that moment, Michael and Lynn entered the room. Lynn headed for the group of gossiping biddies while Michael went to get a drink from Dennis who had taken on his natural role as bartender.

"You would never believe who we ran into sitting outside Melissa's apartment building," she said obviously agitated. "The Gent, can you believe it? We were in shock when we saw him. Michael and I almost walked right past him without noticing, but he looked right at us without recognizing us at first, and said hello. Boy, was he sorry! I called him a scumbag, and then Michael started berating him so he ran off. We were fit to be tied!"

"Who is 'The Gent'?" Katie whispered to Marilyn.

"The lying creep that ran out on Patricia," she murmured back. "It's an unbelievable coincidence."

"He duped us all! If any one of us would have suspected his deviance, we would have done everything in our power to expose him."

"I didn't even meet the sleaze and I hate him," Katie seethed through her teeth.

"Must be a good story," Patricia said as she approached the secretive group. They became tongue tied and didn't answer. "Rabbi and Father Richard had just arrived and they were to bless our home, if you would like to join us."

"Sure," Katie said as she and the others followed Patricia. She now knew why Patricia chose not to discuss her accident.

The Rabbi prayed a blessing in Hebrew and Fr. Richard prayed one in English. Rabbi gave the Callahans a mezuzah as a house warming gift to be placed on the outside post of the front door. The small decorative casing contained scripture blessings from the Torah which were prepared by a qualified scribe in Israel. The priest's housewarming gift was a Celtic holy water font to be placed on the wall next to the inside door. God had them covered coming and going from their home. They already felt truly blessed with the gift of true friendships.

Jack made his way to Katie. "You're little girl is irresistible. I can understand why Robby is so taken with her. I have never seen him so well behaved."

"She has that little motherly gift," she quipped. "I'm surprised she hasn't asked me to leave yet. She's very protective of her father and wanted to stay with him tonight."

"Mommy, are we ready to go yet?" sounded Laura from behind.

"I guess I spoke too soon," Katie said as she winked at Jack who was also very impressed with her.

Katie and Laura said their heartfelt thank-yous and good-byes and headed home.

"Did you have a good time, honey?" she asked Laura on the ride home.

"Oh yes, I just love Robby. He is so cute, mommy. Mrs. Callahan said I can come over anytime and play with Robby and she will pay me. Wait until I tell daddy that I have a job!"

Katie wasn't surprised to find Matt not home when they got there, unlike Laura who insisted something must have happened to him. "Laura, honey, daddy said he was going out with Jim for coffee after the meeting."

"But mommy, he wouldn't be this late."

Katie checked the answering machine to see if anyone called while they were out, and began to agree with Laura when she heard a message from Jim. "Hey Matt, you said you would be waiting outside for me. I've been sitting here for twenty minutes. Sorry Bud, but I gotta go; I don't want to be late for the meeting. I hope everything is all right. I'll call you later."

"I knew I shouldn't have left my daddy," Laura started crying. "I need to go find him."

"Calm down Laura, we'll take a walk after I check with Ann Marie. Maybe he is with her and Kevin."

Katie's initial relief turned to disgust after Ann Marie told her that Matt had just called Kevin, and wanted him to join him at the Irish Pub. Kevin was just about to leave to go get him. "Tell him not to bother. I'm going myself," she said and hung up.

"I'm going with you," Laura emphatically stated.

"You will have to wait outside while I go in to get him or you have to go to Ann Marie's."

"Okay, I'll wait outside."

The two hurried along looking for the Irish Pub. Katie let Laura stay in the foyer where she could see her while she looked around the bar for Matt. She started at one end and made her way to the other but didn't see him. The bar was very dimly lit but she certainly would be able to recognize her own husband. There were some rowdy fellas watching a Celtic football match. At the far end there was a couple making out and groping each other like animals. Katie was surprised the barman didn't throw them out. She was about to leave when Laura ran past her and started screaming "I hate you daddy, I hate you!" She looked to see Laura beating on the lowlife in the corner. Oh my God! It was Matt with that whore! She marched over, looked Matt in the eye and spit in his face, pulling a hysterical Laura away. She could still hear his sick laugh, as she walked out the bar door. The two of them cried all the way home. No words were spoken. They were incapable of relating the nightmare to Ann Marie and Kevin who were on their stoop waiting.

Ann Marie and Kevin immediately hugged them and walked them up to their apartment. They heated some milk for Laura and tea for Katie. Katie didn't want to talk in front of Laura. She felt guilty enough for letting her come and causing her to witness her father's adulterous behavior.

Laura was exhausted from her traumatic ordeal and finally fell asleep on the couch. With Ann Marie's help, Katie immediately packed every bit of Matt's belongings and asked Kevin to deliver them. There would be no more chances or reconciliations for them. She would never get that image of the two kissing and pawing all over each other out of her head. She closed the door on her old life and opened a new one.

THE SUPPORT GROUP

Katie woke up from her lucid nightmare only to realize after a few seconds that it wasn't a nightmare at all. She felt sick to her stomach. Her fairy tale marriage was definitely over. There would be no more waiting or caring if Matt stopped drinking or came to his senses. She would have been able to deal with almost anything but not adultery. She had to find the energy to start a new life for Laura and herself. She began sobbing convulsively into her pillow and didn't realize Laura had climbed into her bed until she felt her little hand stroking her hair to comfort her.

"We'll be all right mommy. We'll have to take care of each other now. I still love my daddy, but in a different way. He did something very mean to you," she said trying to soothe her mother.

Katie lifted her head to look at her amazing daughter and managed a smile. "You're right Laura; it's you and me from now on. I am so sorry that you had to see everything, baby. He'll always be your daddy, honey, but I can't stay married to him anymore." She wanted to make it clear to Laura there was no chance for a reconciliation between Matt and herself.

"It's all my fault," she insisted and started to cry. "I should have stayed home with him."

"Laura, no it's not. It's Daddy's fault. He's the one who started drinking again. We can't babysit him all the time. He was supposed to go to his meeting last night and he didn't go. Honey, something may have happened after we left, but it had nothing to do with you or me." Katie was trying so hard to make her understand.

David was sorry to hear about Matt's drastic setback and told Katie to take all the time she needed to settle things. She insisted that she needed to get back to work as soon as possible. She made an agenda for the day so that she could return to work tomorrow.

She felt a strong need to call Father Seamus. He wasn't shocked, but was sincerely sorry for Katie when she broke down on the phone. "Katie, I am so sorry you are hurting. I prayed it would turn out differently for you and Matt. I've seen the destructive effects of alcohol over and over and I've seen the people and families it destroys. I am sorry I can't change it for you, but it doesn't mean your life is over. You are a strong woman, Kathleen, and you have your life ahead of you. It does disturb me to know that Laura witnessed such shocking behavior and emotional disappointment."

"Father, the child is incredible in the way she appears to rationalize this crazy situation, but I'm concerned because she seems to be holding herself responsible for her father's drinking. She believes that if she stayed home with him, he wouldn't have gotten drunk. His sponsor was supposed to pick him up right after we left, but when he came Matt wasn't here. We have no idea what set him off."

"Katie, it could have been anything. It doesn't matter; he drank. I'm worried about Laura. Alcoholics freely inflict guilt, causing children of alcoholics to naturally assume the guilt which can be harmful to them later in life."

"I'm going to try to make an appointment for both of us to see a family psychologist this afternoon. She is too young for the Al-anon program in our area but we both need talk to someone about it. I know at some time I am going to have to deal with her relationship with her father, but for now I need strength just to survive," she told him honestly as her voice began to crack.

"I am happy that you are both going to get help dealing with this. It's a shame Matt never made an attempt to make it to Sunday Mass with you and Laura. I was hoping he would also seek spiritual assistance," the priest said, clearly disappointed. "Katie, please call me if you need anything, will you?" As an afterthought he asked with concern, "He won't harass or bother you, will he? If he does, don't go soft on him. Alcoholics have to be held accountable for their actions. You do whatever is best for you and Laura."

"I certainly hope he doesn't get nasty! As far as I'm concerned he made his choice when he picked up that first drink last night; I am never getting on that roller coaster with him again. He can ride it alone," she said with an adamant tone. "Father, thank you for listening again and please continue to pray for me, I surely need it." She always felt better after talking to the priest.

She was able to get an appointment with the family psychologist. She felt that she needed it as much if not more than Laura. She just wished it to be already months from now and for the hurt to be over. She strongly believed that time healed all wounds, but only if it would hurry along, so she could get through this. She dreaded the thought of running into Matt and his whore of a girlfriend. She had earlier asked Ann Marie to be the liaison between them if necessary until she retained a lawyer.

Katie felt like an empty zombie all day but managed to tend to Laura and keep the psychologist's appointment. Laura was able to tell Ms. Kim how disappointed and upset she was with her father, but that she still loved him very much. She didn't want to betray her mother but at the same time, she wanted to see her dad sometime in the future and talk to him. Katie expected Laura's loyal devotion to her father, but dreaded having to deal with it. Katie wanted Ms. Kim to help Laura understand that she would be able to see her dad only when he wasn't drinking so that nothing would happen to her and not think that Katie was spitefully keeping her from him. Their first session was a success, despite all the tears.

Later that day Patricia called to offer moral support to Katie. "Why don't you and Laura come for dinner tonight? Robby will surely keep her mind off her father."

"I'll ask her and call you right back. Thank you for being so understanding."

"I've been there myself more than once. Believe me I know the pain."

"It's hell, isn't it?"

"Sure is! But love and friends conquer heartache, believe me, you'll see. I really do hope you can make it tonight."

Katie wasn't up to socializing but Laura was so excited about seeing Robby again. Just before they were leaving for the Callahans, the phone rang and Laura answered, "Daddy, we don't want to talk to you right now. You did something very mean to mommy. We're going out now. Goodbye." She hung up. The phone rang again. Only this time no one answered as mother and daughter closed the door behind them.

Katie was quiet at first, and the Callahans did not want her to feel pressured to talk. Robby kept everyone entertained with his adorable toddler behavior. He insisted on sitting next to Laura. He even pulled her chair out for her to sit. The adults were amazed.

"Where did he ever learn to do that?" asked Katie in disbelief.

"He watches David do that for me," Patricia explained.

"My husband always did nice things like that. In fact some of my friends were jealous of his chivalrous actions toward me," she said in a quivering voice.

After dinner, David insisted on clearing the table so the women could chat. He thought Katie might feel more comfortable talking to Patricia alone. After all, Patricia could identify with spousal betrayal.

"Katie, I was in a diabolical relationship once after David and I separated. We just remarried after being divorced for over six years." She didn't want to divulge anything about David's extramarital affair which had caused their separation because after all David *was* Katie's boss.

"I didn't realize that."

"There was a man I fell for hook, line and sinker. He was tall and gorgeous with impeccable manners. I could take him anywhere and he would fit in. He was a real gentleman chameleon. I really thought I was going to marry him and even move to Hoboken, but" ... Patricia snapped out of her reverie. "Oh, well, like I said I have felt your pain. All my friends rallied around me along with my wonderful husband, and here I am happier than ever. So, Katie, be patient with yourself and let time heal your heart."

"Thank you for caring, Trish. I'm trying to take one day at a time. I think we had better be going now. Laura has school in the morning."

"He won't hurt you, will he? I mean your husband?"

"I have my best friend and my mother nearby. Anyway I'm sure he's busy with his little floozy."

"David is emphatic that you take your time coming back to work; Kjaer is willing to come down temporarily and I can always pitch in and help."

"I need to work and stay busy. It's the best therapy, but thank you for the offer." Katie didn't want to admit that it was a good possibility that Matt might become spiteful and hold back money from her or even lose his job in the near future if he kept on drinking at the rate he was going. "I really want to thank you for a lovely evening. Robby was a great distraction for both Laura and myself," she said managing a smile.

Laura and Robby came walking to the door hand in hand neither one attempting to let go of the other.

"Robby wants to come home with us, Mommy," said Laura as Robby looked up to Katie with pleading eyes. Katie stooped down to him, "Robby, Laura has to go to school tomorrow but you can sleep over another time okay?"

"When?" he asked, delighted.

"Soon," answered his father.

"When soon?" Robby continued the relentless echo of a toddler.

Katie and Laura expressed their thank-yous before they left. The two shared humor in the thought of Robby following Patricia and David around obsessively asking, "when soon?"

The only downside to living in Hoboken was parking or the extreme lack of it. So Katie and Laura had to walk five blocks to their building. They were welcomed by the appalling sight of Matt lying passed out drunk at the bottom of the stairs on the sidewalk. "Daddy," Laura called as she darted toward him but Katie was able to quickly snatch her hand and ran with her into their apartment without waking him.

"Mommy, we can't leave him there," she shouted and started crying.

"I know, Laura, I'm going to call Kevin to come get him. I'm sorry, sweetie, but daddy will NEVER step foot in this apartment again."

"But how can I see him then? He needs me," she continued to sob.

"We'll work something out with Ann Marie for you to see your father when and if he sobers up. Baby, he is not himself right now and could hurt you without really meaning to. Remember when he pushed you and didn't even remember it. Now go get ready for bed and I'll call Kevin." Laura sadly walked into her bedroom. Katie was so angry at Matt for what he was doing to their little girl. His drunken behavior was causing emotional havoc with her and robbing her of a child's peace.

Before she could reach for the phone, "LAURA!!!" was echoing through the streets below. Matt was screaming her name at the top of his drunken lungs. Laura came running from her room. "I heard Daddy calling for me; I need to go to him," she insisted. Katie held her back. "You are not going near him while he's in that condition! Please go stay in your room until Kevin comes for him." Katie went immediately to the window and began spying through the blinds. She thankfully watched a patrol car pull up and two policemen load Matt into the back seat and drive away making her call to Kevin unnecessary.

"It's okay, honey. Daddy left," she called to Laura. "Let's pack a bag for you, I think you should stay at Grandma's tonight." Laura started to object, "Mommy, I want to stay here with you!" but Katie finally convinced her. Katie's mother had a lot of questions about why she wanted Laura to stay there yet again, but Katie told her the answers would have to wait until morning. She stopped next door at Ann Marie's and asked her to take Laura directly to school the next morning. She told her there had been some trouble with Matt but that everything was taken care of for tonight. Katie just wanted to get home.

As soon as she reached the front door, she sensed something was wrong. She was exhausted, and as she put the key into the door she realized it was already opened. She thought it strange that she would have forgotten to lock the door. Oh my God, I have to be more careful, she thought. She had been in such a hurry to get Laura to her grandma's that apparently she hadn't pulled the door shut. She pushed the door open and weakly switched on the light, when she saw Matt slumped in his easy chair grimacing at her and waving Laura's petrified chameleon by its tail.

Before she could take another step, Matt threw the defenseless chameleon against the wall so hard that the poor creature lay on the floor, bleeding profusely.

"Oh my God, Matt, what have you done? Laura loves that chameleon! She is going to be heartbroken!" Katie cried in disbelief.

"I don't like chameleons! She doesn't need it anyway! She has me," he slurred, picking up the bloody creature. With a disgusted look on his face, he tossed it out the window, then fell back on the chair and let out a chilling laugh.

Katie was at an absolute loss. She quickly ran outside to where the chameleon lay, finding that this little creature who had brought such joy to her child was dead. After Matt had initially thrown it against the wall, she still had a vague idea that she would've been able to take it to the vet to be saved, but it was obvious that now it was too late. She had been hoping that over the next few days, Laura's preoccupation with Mattie would divert some of the focus away from the horror of seeing her father passed out in the street. Instead, now Laura would have to deal with the death of her beloved pet. What was she going to tell her? Her mind was racing.

Katie was uncontrollably angry by now and ran back up to the apartment. There was no sign of Matt except for his keys which were lying on the floor where he apparently had haphazardly dropped them. She was going to get the locks changed tomorrow in case he had an extra set.

Katie told Ann Marie that Matt had killed the chameleon and also that she had an idea to avoid poor Laura finding out.

"I'm going to buy another one tomorrow, after all, they frequently change colors and if it doesn't look exactly the same, Laura will never notice."

Ann Marie agreed that this was a good solution. She assured Katie that as planned, she would be bringing Laura to school in the morning and pick her up, so if Katie wanted to get the new chameleon after work she could have it in the tank by the time she brought Laura home.

Katie was wide awake into the wee hours of the morning. She sensed that she was not going to able to control or stop Matt's unexpected or irrational visits without leaving her most favorite place in the world and her home – Hoboken.

David was alarmed when he saw the condition of Katie upon walking into her office. Her eyes were red and swollen. She was a million miles away and didn't see him, so he quietly left so as not to disturb her. He was not very savvy in handling women's affairs which prompted him to call Patricia immediately to relate his concern. She insisted on coming right to the office.

Katie appreciated Patricia's impromptu visit to the office. She needed to share the latest events with someone, and hadn't been able to talk properly with Ann Marie or her mother before work. She didn't want to overburden Ann Marie while she was enjoying the newness of a budding relationship with Kevin. Katie was all cried out and emotionally depleted. She was able to share the latest news with Patricia without sobbing.

"You may need a restraining order against him, Katie," Patricia suggested.

"I am hoping to amicably dissuade him from inciting any further craziness. Although I keep reminding myself that I am now dealing with a diseased man whose thought process is influenced by alcohol."

"Have you thought of moving?" Patricia said without realizing Katie's strong emotional ties to Hoboken. The suggestion evoked tears in Katie's eyes.

"That may be a strong possibility in order to provide Laura with peace and security but Hoboken has been my childhood paradise. I always wanted Laura to have the opportunity to experience a close knit community like I did," she sighed.

"I've heard that about Hoboken," she said in a sardonic tone that caused Katie to raise her eyebrows.

When Patricia was reassured that Katie was in better form, she went to report to David who was entertaining Robby in his office. David was concerned about Katie's situation after Patricia's revelation and thought she needed more time off, but Patricia insisted work was the best remedy at a time like this. She herself had learned that firsthand.

"I think I'll check for available apartments near us just in case she decides to move. I've been looking for a new project."

"You really are a wonderful caring person," he said as he pulled her into her arms and kissed her passionately.

"I don't know why but I feel a strong connection and camaraderie with Katie right now. But she is genuinely a lovely person. But I'd better get our little fellow home for his nap," Patricia said as they watched Robby's eyes begin to droop while he sat cock-eyed on the chair.

The next few weeks or so had been without any incidents. Katie and Laura went to their weekly family therapy sessions, and seemed to be adjusting as best they could. They spent a lot of time with Ann Marie, Suzie and Kevin. Katie considered no news from Matt as good news. She had met with her lawyer to begin the divorce proceedings. Katie wanted to get her life organized. She found the constant anxiety of the uncertainty very troublesome. She was having Matt served with divorce papers at work, since she had no idea where he was staying. She didn't want to make Kevin her carrier pigeon for information and have him caught in the middle of their failed and possibly volatile relationship.

The peaceful hiatus wasn't to last long before Katie received a call from Laura's school. Apparently a very drunken Matt *and* a less than modestly dressed woman who was also obnoxiously inebriated showed up at Laura's school demanding to see her. The school principal was wise enough to call the police immediately, as well as Katie. Matt had evidently staggered into the school shouting through the halls to see his daughter, Laura Reilly. The whole school went into lockdown. The principal assured her that Matt was in police custody at the moment but that Laura was upset over the whole charade. He also reassured Katie that everything was now under control but suggested that she come and get an emotional Laura. He also wanted to meet with her at a later time to discuss the family situation in order to keep Laura and the other children safe from any further visits by Matt to the school. Katie felt humiliated, after all, she was still married to this drunken derelict. She left work immediately after explaining the new Matt crisis to David. It was now time for a restraining order, decided an angry and embarrassed Katie. She was furious not only that he made a scene at the school, but that he brought that cartoon character of a slut with him!

Laura was relieved when her mother picked her up early from school. Katie wanted to be truthful with her daughter without alarming her so she explained to her that her father's drinking was spiraling out of control, and she had to take action to protect them until he sobered up. Katie felt it important that Laura understand that a drunken Matt was not the affectionate, loving daddy Laura had once known, but tried to explain that he could be if he stopped drinking. They went to Ann Marie's to wait for Suzie to get home from school. Katie and Laura both needed their best friends right now.

Patricia berated David for not calling her when Katie abruptly left work. She felt she needed someone with her for moral support. She called Katie's cell after not reaching her at home. "Katie, is everything okay?"

"For now, I guess. I'm just so spent. I have life-changing decisions to make and I feel so confused at the moment," she said in exasperation.

"I'd like to be there with you and Laura. I can pick up dinner for us," she offered.

"Actually I am at my friend Ann Marie's home, if you'd like to come over. I certainly can use all the moral support I can get right now but don't worry about dinner. We can order something when you get here. I feel as if you are a special angel that God has sent me," she professed.

"I feel the same about you, and I am looking forward to meeting Ann Marie," Patricia returned.

She looked again at Ann Marie's address and directions that Katie had given her and felt a sudden shudder looking at the Hoboken address. She had once dreamed about living there happily ever after. What was it about that city that still gave her an ominous feeling despite the warm and fuzzy nostalgia people talked about?

The ride was directly off Route 3 as Katie had stated. Her directions had been dead on. She found Ann Marie's house with no trouble and lucked out with a parking spot right outside her home. She pictured Hoboken a bit differently but appreciated its unique charm. She couldn't help but wonder if Matt lived nearby or if he had since moved. She was also curious about his wife. What kind of woman would be married to a chameleon like him? Did he fool her like he had herself? Her thoughts were interrupted when the door was answered by Laura. She had run to the door expecting to see Robby. "Sorry, honey but I came alone," she told her. "I didn't dare tell him that I was coming. I needed a night out alone but next time he can come with me."

"Is he still asking 'when soon'?" Laura giggled at the thought of his determination for a definite answer about coming to her house.

Laura led her into the kitchen to see her mom and to meet Ann Marie. They were sitting at the kitchen table drinking tea while they waited for her. "I wish you would have called me from outside so I could have helped you in. I completely forgot about the stairs. I'm so sorry, Patricia," she said as she kissed her hello.

"I'm fine. I'm getting better at it. Practice makes perfect."

"I'm Ann Marie. I am so glad to meet you. Katie has told me so much about you."

"Likewise," answered Patricia.

Laura ran back to continue playing The Barbie Game with Suzie while the women got acquainted and formed their new support group. The women bonded over a pizza and a bottle of Chianti while each shared their own prior disappointments with men. Ann Marie and Patricia knew only too well the feelings of betrayal and abandonment that Katie was now experiencing.

Katie announced that the only solution she could find to protect herself and Laura from any further embarrassment or abuse from Matt was to move. She had it all thought out. Matt was never to know where they were moving, and Ann Marie's home would be the pick-up and drop-off spot for Laura if a sober Matt wanted time with her in the future. Although her role was presumptuous by Katie, Ann Marie was only too glad to help. The realization that her best friend was possibly thinking of moving away saddened her tremendously and she began to cry.

"Ann Marie, I don't think I have any other recourse," Katie quivered. "I need peace for Laura and myself. Besides, I have to worry about my parents. I hope he leaves them alone and doesn't start harassing them."

"Too late," Katie's parents announced as they entered the kitchen. It was the norm for the two families to walk into each other's homes at any time unannounced. "Katie, we saw your car here so we came over to tell you about the crazy phone call that we just received from Matt," said her mother.

"Katie, my God, what is going on with you and Matt?" her father asked.

"Ssshh. Please, I don't want the girls to hear. Laura has been through so much already," Katie whispered.

Patricia, feeling a bit intrusive, excused herself, but not before she quickly introduced herself to Katie's parents. She thought Katie would feel more comfortable with less people around while she explained her bizarre dilemma. Katie walked her to her car this time.

"Thank you so much for coming," she said as she helped her into her car.

"You are more than welcome. If there is anything I can do, please ask. I was thinking that I can scout out some apartments in our area just in case you decide you want to move to that area," Patricia offered.

"That would be great, since it looks like the prospect is inevitable. Especially since the fool is now bothering my parents. How much more of my life is that moron going to disrupt? I really can't believe this is happening to me," she said in exasperation.

"Don't worry Katie; you have a good family and wonderful friends to help you through this. Believe me, you will get through this. Time will be your best friend. You'll see," she said with a strong voice of experience.

Katie tried to smile through her tears as they began to roll down her cheeks. "Thank you. I'll try to remember that," she said as she closed Patricia's car door and turned toward Ann Marie's house. How she dreaded going back in and having to tell her parents about the whole charade she had been living for the past months. She decided to leave out some incidents like the sight of Matt and that woman in the bar and the tragic death of Mattie.

She wasn't surprised to find that Ann Marie's parents had now joined the pow-wow in her kitchen. They lived in the upstairs apartment of the two family house shared with Ann Marie and Suzie. She explained the past months of hell filled with Matt's drunken abuse and the attempts to reconcile after the accident, when he seemed willing to quit. Of course she gave them the much-abridged version. She quickly left the shocked group on the note that she would be moving as quickly as possible in order to avoid any more detriment to herself and Laura.

However, they were not surprised that there was trouble in the marriage. After all, Laura was staying with them a lot more often in the last few months. They were not exactly sure of their suspicions until Katie started working. They were just waiting for her to tell them when she was ready. They didn't want to add anymore anxiety to their daughter's life.

LꜲURꜲ'S VISIT

This is where I belong, mused Katie as she sat captivated by the New York Skyline while sitting on a park bench at the Hoboken waterfront facing the City. She had always found serenity here while she listened to the familiar sounds of human activity. How she missed the social racket of the joggers' pounding feet on the path as they ran past, the boisterous toots of little tugboats calling attention to their impressive feat of pulling massive cruise ships out of the harbor, the loud sounds of helicopters whizzing through the air up and down the river, and the recreational boats sailing at different speeds through the waterway causing breaking waves to crash against the piers. She often wondered what the many tourists lining the decks of the sightseeing ferries thought of this delightful paradise.

Katie always made it a point to visit this blissful spot when she returned to Hoboken. It was already two years since she and Laura had moved to Cedar Grove. Patricia found them a lovely apartment a mile away from the Callahan home. They were pretty settled now in their new environment. Laura's family-oriented school, St. Catherine's, was only two blocks away from their new place. Patricia insisted on picking Laura up every day after school. She maintained that she needed her to watch Robby and even paid Laura, while refusing to take any money from Katie. Robby and Laura had created a special bond that amazed the adults. Strangers assumed that they were brother and sister based on their similar looks and mannerisms.

Katie had just dropped Laura off at Ann Marie's so that a sober Matt could take her for the day. It was the first time they would see each other, since the night he passed out outside the apartment and then killed Mattie. Katie refused his many pleas to talk or meet which were constantly being presented to her by Ann Marie. She had become their personal carrier pigeon. Matt and Laura had an on-again, off-again telephone relationship when Matt wasn't drinking. Laura knew the rules of not divulging any information of where she went to school or where they lived and definitely not their home telephone number. Katie had gotten a cell phone for Laura only when she was sure that Laura was wise enough to know when Matt was drunk. He would call her hysterically crying about how much he missed his little girl. Her cell number was changed already many times because of his on and off the wagon escapades. It was an expensive but necessary price to pay for peace of mind. Katie accepted Laura's illusion of hope that Matt would remain sober this time. Despite warnings from Katie and their family psychologist, Laura believed that she could be an inspirational remedy to his malady, if she could spend some quality time with him when he was sober. They were afraid she was setting herself up for another huge disappointment.

Matt was on a short ride to hell. He had moved in with Nikki, his 'prostitute girlfriend' as Katie called her.

"Well she certainly looked and acted the part," opined Katie even though she had only seen her once. Kevin had advised Katie that Matt was fired for going to work drunk and for refusing employee assistance. She couldn't believe that he had thrown away that great- paying job. She was happy that she had made herself financially self-sufficient, and provided Laura with a comfortable life-style. She had not asked or counted on Matt for any support after their permanent separation. Katie was granted a divorce after numerous no-shows from Matt to court. He was furious when he learned that the divorce went through despite his stall tactics. Katie also learned that he had been arrested and spent the night in jail for causing a physical fight in the Irish Pub from which he was now barred. Nikki bailed him out the next day and the two happily sought out a new watering hole.

Father Seamus was disappointed that Matt was not willing to work the AA program as he should have done during his short breaks from drinking. Katie was thankful that she had taken the AA priest's advice regarding a tough love approach in dealing with Matt. She couldn't imagine what her life would possibly be like if she had stayed with him. She had gone on with her life without him and really was doing alright now.

She returned her attention to her present setting at the bustling waterfront. She swore to move back someday regardless of when or how. She heard Ann Marie shouting her name and turned to see her running toward her. She was out of breath and panting when she reached Katie. "Katie, Laura called crying," she blurted out." C'mon, we have to go get her. She's waiting outside Matt's apartment."

"What happened? What did he do to her?" she shrieked, as she started running to Ann Marie's illegally parked car, leaving Ann Marie struggling to keep up.

They found Laura standing at the curb still sobbing. She ran into Katie's arms. "I'm never coming back here. I hate that lady," she shouted.

Matt had been watching Katie consoling Laura from his living room window. He was overcome not only with a pang of guilt but also a strong heartache from seeing Katie again. He didn't even realize that he'd murmured, "Oh, Katie," until Nikki came up from behind and sneered, "I'm your lady now."

"YOU are no lady!" he spat at her.

"You can't talk to me that way!" she screamed.

"Oh yes I can," he said through clenched teeth. "I finally get to see my daughter and you get jealous and try to compete with her. You tell her that I killed her pet! Are you crazy?" he seethed. He slapped her across the face.

"How dare you!" She shouted at him slapping him right back before storming out of the apartment.

Katie and Laura were gone by the time he returned to the window. He left and went out to the nearest bar to restart his destructive cycle. Coincidentally, he and Nikki both had the same agenda after their physical altercation and headed for the same bar, Doc's. The place was a real dump and stunk of stale beer. It was not just dimly lit; it was dark. The light fixtures were very old as was everything else in the place. The floor was caked with dirt and the walls and ceiling wore the old residue of stale smoke. The mirrors were grimy and shattered in places where patrons had thrown their empty glasses. This was their watering hole, and the two enjoyed the benefits of the cheap booze with the company of lonely old men who had no other friend than their drinks.

Matt walked in to see Nikki crying on the shoulder of a drunken old man with a sympathetic ear. "I thought he was different from all the rest," she cried. "He treated me like a lady and his best friend. We did everything together. I really thought he was the one, my knight in shining armor," she further sobbed. Matt felt like the biggest heel and walked out. He had misled Nikki too. He decided it was time to end the charade. He went in search of help, by immediately calling his A.A. sponsor, who convinced him to enter an alcohol rehab center.

Meanwhile, Katie held Laura and kissed the top of head while she calmed down. "Tell mommy what happened, baby," she cooed softly.

"That lady didn't like me sitting on daddy's lap. She said that I was too old to act like that," she sniveled.

"What did daddy say?"

"He told her to shut up. She had the nerve to sit down on the couch right next to us. She was almost sitting on daddy's lap too. Daddy told her that he was taking me out for lunch alone, just the two of us; she got *really* mad. When Daddy went to the bathroom before we left, she started laughing like a witch and told me..." she became emotional and spurted out, "*she* told me that Daddy killed Mattie and that you must have bought me another chameleon."

"Oh baby, I'm so sorry. I didn't want you to find out. That's why I bought you a new Mattie. Daddy felt really sorry when he sobered up." Katie couldn't believe she found herself still making excuses for Matt.

"Did he really? But I still can't believe daddy did that," and she began to cry again.

Katie looked over Laura's head at Ann Marie, and they both pursed their lips in anger at Matt for telling that insensitive sleaze that he killed his daughter's pet.

"I never want to see that ugly lady again! She wears too much makeup anyway."

The two women almost had to laugh at Laura's quick perception of Nikki's shallowness. Katie was afraid that this incident was going to set Laura back emotionally. You did it again Matt, she thought to herself. By the time they got to Ann Marie's there was a message on her phone from Matt asking her to extend his apologies to Laura, since she had turned her cell off signaling that she was mad at him. It didn't surprise Katie when a week later Laura was back talking to Matt. She overheard her pleading with him for the best birthday present in the world – to have her sober daddy back again. Katie felt her heart strings pull from Laura's words, but after all, Matt still had several months to accommodate her wish.

LAURA'S PARTY

The Callahans' perfectly manicured yard was decorated beautifully for Laura's surprise birthday party. Katie had rented four large round tables and draped them in Laura's favorite colors, pink and lavender. The tables boasted metallic centerpieces that hoisted balloons into the air. Not much decorating needed to be done since the yard bloomed with magnificent colors. The floral atmosphere yielded a peaceful seclusion to the outside world. The caterer was busy setting up the chafing dishes and accessories while Katie was seeing to the last minute details. Patricia walked out of the sliding doors onto the Belgian blocked patio with Robby in tow. "Mommy, do you think Laura will let me help her open her presents?"

Overhearing this from inside, David was quick to call, "Please come here, son. I need to talk to you," he said, stooping down to take both of Robby's hands in his own. Looking him straight in the eyes he said, "I want you to remember that this is Laura's party and not yours. I want you to behave yourself today or I am going to take away your bicycle for a week. It's your decision." Robby pouted as he weighed the ultimatum, but David knew there was no contest when it came to Robby and his bicycle. While most children nowadays seemed to prefer to stay indoors and play video games, his son chose to explore the outdoors. He was a child with an extremely creative imagination that enabled him to transform his daily rides into space adventures or some sort of exciting exploration.

"Okay, Dad, I know the rules. I'll try to be a gentleman and mind my manners. *"But,* if Laura *asks* me to help her, can I?" he asked in a boyish plea. David gave him a skeptical look as he said in a warning tone, *"only* if she asks you!" As he got older, Robby was learning how to manipulate people, including his parents, with his charming manner. David and Patricia found their son's diplomatic appeal endearing, although they wanted to be sure he was always considerate of other people. He was the apple of their eye as well as their greatest joy in life.

"I can't thank you enough for helping me with this party, Trish," Katie said sincerely.

"Katie, don't be silly," Patricia said as she hugged her. "You know how much we love you and Laura. You've become like family to us. Our lives have become so enriched by your friendship. I hope Laura will be surprised. By the way, I meant to ask you if you ever reached her father."

"I did, and he's coming. Ann Marie and Kevin are bringing him. Believe me, he is going to be her best birthday present ever! Even though seeing him again still disturbs me, I know Laura loves him more than anything. They have always had a special bond and I respect that. I told him to come a little later than the other guests only because once he is here she won't have eyes or time for anyone else."

"You really are a wonderful mother, Katie."

"I try. Well, I'd better go fetch our little birthday princess. Trish, you won't forget to call me when most of the guests are here," Katie said anxiously.

"Don't worry, I won't forget, not with Robby here to remind me every five seconds," Patricia laughed. "Oh, and Jack is going to be late. He's working overtime today. He insisted that I tell you that he doesn't want to miss seeing the princess on her birthday."

"Now that is a real gentleman for you," Katie responded as she hurried away to speak with Laura.

Laura was overwhelmed with shock when she entered the Callahans' backyard. The shouts of "*SURPRISE!*" rang through her ears. Shocked and thrilled, she was shaking with the excitement. Within moments, tears of joy were rolling down her face. She kissed and hugged her mom as Katie placed a tiara upon her head. "Mommy, I love you so much," she said as they walked arm and arm further into the yard.

Robby was the first one to run up and greet Laura. "I kept a good secret, didn't I, Laura?" he boasted proudly.

"You sure did," she answered as she squeezed him tightly.

Laura made the rounds to see all of her guests. Her grand-mother Kathy was sitting with Robby's grandma, Isleen who flew up from Florida especially for Laura's party. She had become very fond of Laura and Katie over the last few years. She considered them to be extended family just as Patricia and David did. Laura had a special rapport with Robby and had a wonderful way of entertaining him.

Ann Marie's parents, Karen and Liam were sitting with the grandmothers. They had known Laura since she was born and shared in much of her life. Suddenly, Suzie sprang up from behind her grandparents' chairs shouting, "Surprise!"

Laura ran over to her and grabbed her hands as they began to jump up and down shrieking.

"Your mom asked me to sleep over tonight!" she blurted with excitement.

"Oh, what a great birthday present," Laura cried.

Robby stood by pouting as though he had been left out. "Laura, can I be your birthday present too?" he asked, on the verge of tears.

Laura rushed to him and hugged him tightly. "Robby, ask your mommy if you can sleep over with us too," she said affectionately. "This way I can be with my two best birthday presents."

"Oh boy, can I?" he shouted as he hugged her and then quickly ran to find his mother.

"I hope you don't mind Suzie, but I love him so much. He's like the little brother I've always wanted," Laura said apologetically.

"Of course I don't mind. He really is so cute. I can certainly understand why you are so fond of him."

The grandparents had been observing the interactions between the children. "They are three lovely children," said Grandma Isleen. "I find the resemblance between Laura and Robby to be uncanny. They could pass as siblings."

"They may as well be since they are always together," added Grandma Elizabeth. Laura continued to greet her guests with Suzie and Robby, who was back in tow.

Katie was busy uncovering the chafing dishes when she heard that dreaded squeal, "Daddy, Oh Daddy *you're* here." She turned to see Laura running into her father's arms and quickly turned away trying to compose herself. She looked to Patricia for emotional support. The moment she caught her eye, Patricia's face had turned white as snow. She watched Patricia's legs give out as she swooned to the ground. Katie and David ran to her as she came to. She was so relieved that everyone's attention was focused on Laura and Matt and not her.

"Are you all right, Love?" David asked with great concern.

"Are you hurt?" Katie asked.

"Please can you both help me upstairs quickly? I am so embarrassed. I guess I just got a bit overly excited about today, but I'll be fine if I lay down a while."

The two supported her, one on either side, and walked her into the house and up the stairs. Once in her bedroom, she apologized to the both of them. "I am so sorry. I guess my legs gave way." Katie wasn't too quick to believe it. Not after witnessing the look on Patricia's face at the exact moment she had seen Matt. This was not the time or place to question what she had observed but her interest was piqued.

"You both go back to the party. I'll be okay after a nap." David would not leave her until he was convinced for himself. Katie agreed that one of them should be at the party. She assured Patricia she would be up to check on her later. She really wanted to know if it was the sight of Matt that made Patricia faint. Could it possibly be just a coincidence? She didn't think so, not really. It was too difficult for Katie to process this right now; a lot of things were going through her head.

"Hi Katie," Matt said as he walked toward her. "You look more beautiful than I remember." He kissed her on the cheek.

"Thank you, but Matt, I can't…"

"Please Katie, hear me out," he said in a pleading tone. "I haven't had a drink in six months. I left Nikki in a bar and signed into a rehab. I swear. I even go to AA meetings almost every night," he said, hoping to convince her of his newly found sobriety. He wanted so badly to win her approval.

"You're just a little too late." Katie started to walk away, but he quickly blocked her path.

"Please, I am really working on my AA steps, and I need to make my amends to a lot of people but most of all to you, Katie. There are things I need to tell you in order for me to help myself. I really need to do this, especially for Laura. Would you be willing to come to Hoboken for dinner during the week? My treat," he added quickly with his charming smile.

Katie looked into his eyes for the first time in a long time and saw a sincerity she hadn't seen in years. She still thought him good-looking despite the wrinkles and early aging from his excessive drinking. She sensed that he was nervous by his incessant habit of twisting his hands together like a scared schoolboy. She realized how hard his recovery from drinking must be for him. Laura had told her that Matt sounded sober on his regular calls to her, but Katie thought it was Laura's wishful thinking. She wanted to help him, especially for Laura's sake, but she didn't want to get hurt again. She didn't want to step back into his dysfunctional world. She had protected Laura as much as she could from it. They were content with their lives; despite Katie's feelings and pangs of loneliness now and then. Jack was beginning to fill that void for her. They would sometimes go out with Ann Marie and Kevin though the relationship hadn't progressed much past the friendship stage. She wasn't sure if she wanted to get involved with another man, although she knew that they were strongly attracted to each other.

"All right, give me a call during the week, and we'll see if I can make it," she yielded. He still had a way of charming her and getting his way.

"Thanks Kates, You still mean the world…." His over-the-top sentiment was cut off abruptly as Laura ran up to them waving her camera.

"Mommy and Daddy, can we take a picture together for the birthday album Ann Marie and Suzie are going to put together for me?"

"I tell you what, sweetheart, what if I take a picture of you and Daddy together?" Katie didn't want to encourage Laura into thinking there was going to be any sort of reunion.

Laura sighed but agreed. After all, she respected her mother's feelings since she had witnessed much of the hurt that her father had caused. She had heard Katie cry herself to sleep many nights. Regardless, her father was still her hero and she would always love him.

Just as Katie was snapping the photo of Matt and Laura, Robby quickly stepped in on the other side of Matt before anyone could stop him. Robby turned to Matt and asked, "Are you really Laura's Daddy?"

"Yes I am. And who are you, young man?" Matt questioned.

"I'm Robby and I'm her boyfriend," he said emphatically as he reached across and took her hand.

"He usually tells people he's my little brother," she whispered to Matt. "He told me that his father warned him that he had better act like a gentleman today or he'd lose his bike for a week."

"He certainly is fond of you, sweetheart," Matt observed.

"I love him to pieces. He's the little boy I've been telling you about."

"Oh, the one who you've been babysitting for a while now," he recalled.

"Yes, I wish I had a baby brother just like him," she sighed.

"I'm sorry, princess. I guess that's my fault," Matt admitted.

"It's okay, Daddy. I still love you no matter what." Matt hugged her with all his strength. She had always meant the world to him and she was all he had right now.

"We'll get a picture of just the two of us later," Matt assured her. And, afterwards, they did manage to get one without Robby ever noticing.

Katie turned to see Matt on all fours giving Robby a horsey ride. She was quick to snap that picture. The tender scene brought back memories of when Laura was younger.

David joined Katie and assured her that Patricia was fine. "She's going to sleep awhile but feels really terrible about missing Laura's party," he said.

"She shouldn't think that, after making all this possible. I'll go check on her later myself," Katie told him. She still wasn't sure if she could have misread Patricia's reaction to Matt upon his arrival but was determined to find out.

"If I didn't know better, I would think he was a nice guy," David said looking in Matt's direction.

"He was the best at one time but that was a long time ago," Katie admitted.

They watched as Matt was running around the yard with Robby on his shoulders like a bull charging after Laura and Suzie. Robby was giggling and having the time of his life. Matt was having a good time too. He hadn't enjoyed himself like this in very a long time. He was out of breath by the time it came to singing Happy Birthday to Laura. He whispered to Katie, "I don't think I would be able to blow out those candles if I had to right now." She smiled at the thought. Matt was glad that she had finally given him a positive response.

"By the way, where's David's wife?" Matt asked.

"She's lying down. She nearly fainted right after you walked into the yard," Katie said, not sure if she was telling the truth or not.

"I was looking forward to meeting her after everything Laura has told me about her. She assured me that I would like her."

"I know, and it really is a shame she can't be at this party after all she did to help me arrange it."

"I just met David and he seems like a great guy," Matt said.

"He certainly is, and a wonderful boss too," Katie lauded.

"Are you happy, Katie?"

"I wouldn't say that I am *happy*, but I am content."

"Hey, Matt, are you ready to go?" Kevin asked, unaware of the intimate moment he was interrupting.

"Do I have to?" he asked, staring into Katie's eyes. She broke the gaze, thanked him for coming and walked away. There was a lot of cleanup work to be done. Suzie kissed her mom and grandparents good-bye and followed to help Katie.

"Wait a sec," Matt said as he started back toward the yard. He couldn't think of leaving without saying good-bye and thanking David. He found him helping the girls with the yard cleanup.

"David, I didn't want to leave without telling you that it was a pleasure meeting you. I sincerely want to thank you for being so good to Laura and Katie. I really do love them. I only wish I had it to do it all over again."

"Matt, we all make mistakes. I was *lucky* to be given a second chance. I wish the same for you." They shook hands and as Matt walked away, David thought how different Matt was from the way he had perceived him to be. He certainly hadn't expected to like Katie's ex. In fact, if he'd been asked before today he would have said quite the opposite.

Meanwhile, Matt and Laura started toward Kevin's car when Robby snuck up and took Matt's other hand.

"We see that you have a new friend, Matt," Ann Marie quipped as Robby beamed.

"When are you coming back to play with me?" Robby asked Matt.

"Whenever your mommy and daddy say it is okay, I'll come back."

"Goody! Goody!" Robby chanted as he jumped up and down.

"Excuse me, Robby, but he's my daddy," Laura chided him.

"You're supposed to share. Don't I share my daddy with you?" he reminded her. She hugged and kissed the little boy.

"Hey, save some of those kisses for me, princess," Matt griped, pretending to be jealous. Laura ran to his arms and smothered his face with kisses just like she did when she was a little girl.

As Matt stepped into the car, he glanced back at the house hoping to get a last glimpse of Katie. He was disappointed to see she was nowhere in sight, but he thought he saw someone peering from an upstairs window. It was probably a street light's reflection on the window, he thought as he closed the car door. He looked back again to wave to Laura as they drove away. How he wished he could turn back time to when he, Katie, and Laura were a happy family.

Patricia watched him from the upstairs window. She felt emotionally torn as she looked at Matt from afar. He really was all mine at one time, all mine, she thought. He had to have loved me. He was so attentive to me and instinctively knew how a woman liked to be treated. I don't believe all of it was a lie. For that one wonderful month he was my Prince Charming.

Jack pulled up just in time to see Matt getting into Kevin's car. He watched in shock as they pulled off. He sprang from his car in a panic and ran to the backyard shouting for Patricia.

"Where's Patricia?" he asked Katie in a frenzy as she started toward him.

"She's lying down," Katie answered, quite bewildered by Jack's unexpected behavior.

"What did that bastard do to her?" he shouted, adding, "I'll kill him!"

"No one hurt Patricia. She fainted earlier so we helped her to bed." She looked Jack in the eye. "And who are you talking about?"

"The Gent! That despicable creature, Matt Reilly, that's who!" he spit out with undisguised vehemence. "I just saw him getting into the car. By the way, how do you know him? Why was *he* here?" he quickly grilled her.

"Because he's Laura's father," she answered quietly still processing Jack's inexplicable anger. Katie's head began to swirl as she began to repeat Jack's words in her mind. Matt, Patricia's "Gent"? No! He couldn't be that horrible creature everyone referred to! Unable to process the shocking news, she began to swoon and fell to the ground before Jack could reach for her.

David had just stepped onto the patio in time to watch Katie drop to the ground. "My God, what is making our women faint today?" he asked as he rushed to help Jack.

"You mean *WHO*, not what! Were you aware that you were entertaining Matt Reilly today?" he asked in a facetious manner.

"Matt, yeah, Laura's dad," he said in a so-what tone.

"You mean the *gent,*" Jack clarified.

David continued to look at him puzzled; he was unaware of the code name all their friends and relatives used when talking about Matt. "What *are* you talking about?" he asked, totally baffled.

"Matt is Robby's biological father," he announced, unaware that Katie had come to, just in time to overhear them.

"Oh my God! He was in my backyard playing with *my* son! That explains why Patricia fainted when she saw him!" David continued to ramble his thoughts aloud. "I thought it was strange that she stayed in bed this whole afternoon... she would have never have wanted to miss Laura's party!"

The two men were interrupted by soft sobs coming from a grief-stricken Katie who was still half on the ground. She managed to lift herself up. "I need to talk to Patricia alone," she said adamantly, as they helped her to her feet.

"Katie, I am so sorry that you had to find out this way. I never meant to hurt you, but I feel so responsible for Patricia. After all, I was the one who introduced them to each other," Jack quietly explained. "I thought it was a great idea at the time because he told us that he wasn't married."

"I understand," she said. She started toward the house.

"Do you want me to come with you?" David asked with concern.

"No, I need a little time with her alone please," she answered.

"She really was clueless about that chameleon," David said sadly. The two men remained in the yard talking more about Matt and how he had duped Patricia. David felt the old anger flaring up again. He was also feeling extraordinarily sad. Matt was again in their lives.

"I always wanted to know what kind of naive woman Matt Reilly was married to," Jack commented. "I would have never guessed anyone like Katie. Boy, he really was a chameleon."

"Chameleon is right! I actually thought he seemed like a decent guy! Jack, do you think he will try to cause any more trouble or unhappiness in our lives? I hope he stays away… I'll do whatever it takes to protect my family."

Katie stood in the doorway to Patricia's room and watched as she sat with her legs dangling over the side of the bed. She was totally engrossed with something that she held in her hands and did not hear Katie approach. Katie now knew who was responsible for Patricia's sordid tragedy. The creep that befriended Patricia, lived off her for a time, never told her that he was married, then just up and left with no warning, was none other than Matt! Katie gently sat on the bed next to her and looked at the object of her reverie before Patricia quickly tried to hide it. It was a picture of Matt and Patricia dressed in 1700's garb, apparently taken at the Mystic Seaport.

"I know everything, Patricia," she said in a muffled voice, trying unsuccessfully to hold back tears. As soon as the words were out of her mouth, she began to sob uncontrollably. She repeated herself, a little more firmly this time. "I know it all now. What Matt did to you...oh God, what he did to me..." as her words faded, Patricia instinctively put an arm around Katie. She wanted to provide solace to a heart broken by the same man who had broken her own. There was so much these two women could say to each other but neither wanted to speak right now. They each had their own feelings of betrayal to deal with.

The men helped Suzie and Laura pack Robby's overnight bag while the women were trying their best to compose themselves.

The children burst into the bedroom with David and Jack right behind them. "Bye, Mommy, I'm going to sleep at Laura's house," he said as he climbed upon the bed to give his mother a kiss and a hug before he left. Laura bent over at the side of the bed to kiss Patricia also. "I missed you at my party," she said. "Thank you so much. I was so surprised," she added.

"Yeah, Mommy, she cried twice, when she saw her party, and then when her daddy came. I like him. He said he would come back and play with me if you and daddy say it's okay," he informed the room. The adults cringed, sickened by his words. They quickly changed the subject.

"C'mon children let's go." David looked at Robby. "Come now, your mom needs her rest." David herded the kids from the room, so he could provide some assistance to Katie getting them settled in the car. He felt strongly that he needed to get a good night hug from his precocious son. He was wondering if letting Robby spend the night at Katie's was even a good idea now that they all knew the score. It felt awkward to say anything and he kept it to himself. Jack hung back a minute to speak with Patricia.

"I am so sorry for the pain I caused today."

"Jack, you didn't do anything. What are you talking about?"

"It was me who revealed who Matt really was to David. And Katie overheard me say that he was Robby's biological father!"

"Jack, you were only looking out for me, as you always have." Patricia stretched up to kiss his cheek. Jack turned away, feeling embarrassed. He quickly mumbled his goodbye and left the room with his head down.

Patricia was relieved to be alone again. How could this possibly be, she thought. How ironic! Poor Katie! She sat up and took the picture from underneath the covers and began reminiscing again. She didn't realize that David was standing over her and looking at the picture also.

"What do you want to do about this?" he asked hesitantly.

"Nothing, he was a big unexpected shock, that's all. I don't want to see him ever again and I absolutely don't want him near Robby ever again," she said, clenching her teeth. She tore up the picture in one violent move. "I'll discuss that with Katie tomorrow, but I don't want Robby staying over there tonight. I want him here with us."

"I didn't want to let him go but when you didn't say anything I didn't want to upset you. I'll go over and get him right now. I am sure Katie will totally understand. I can't imagine her wanting him there right now anyway after learning who his father is...looking at him will just remind her constantly of what happened."

"Please go get him. Tell him I'm sick and that I'm crying for him. You know what a mush he can be when I'm not well."

"I'll be right back with *our* son," David averred. He held her tightly and laid her back on the bed. He wasn't sure he wanted to let go.

David returned shortly with a sleeping Robby already in his pajamas. "He went out like a light as soon as I turned the first corner," David told Patricia, who had been anxiously waiting.

"Was he upset about leaving?"

"No, he told them that he would be back after he came home and gave you a kiss."

"How is Katie?"

"Gracious, as always. She kept looking at Robby and smiling like she was reliving a memory. She totally understood why we wanted him with us. I think she was actually relieved," he whispered to Patricia, as they tucked the little boy into his bed. "Let's try and get some sleep."

During the night while David was holding Patricia, she suddenly pulled away from him and moved to the other side of the bed. He watched her writhe in her sleep. He was robbed of his own sleep that night as he relived the entire Matt and Patricia story over and over again in his mind. He kept seeing Matt's face and then Robby's. He realized that Patricia had never even mentioned that incredible resemblance. Damn it, Robby was *his* son, physical appearance aside. He and Patricia had come so far since then but he couldn't help wondering if Matt's "resurrection" would affect their relationship.

The next morning Patricia advised David that she needed time away to think. "Please don't leave me," he pleaded with tears in his eyes as he held her tightly.

"I'm not leaving you, David. I wish you would understand that I feel an urgent need to get away for a while." Realizing he had no choice, he released her and walked out of the room. He desperately felt as though his life was crumbling around him. He was devastated at the possibility of losing Patricia and Robby. He wanted so badly to go in search of Matt and beat the hell out of him. Unfortunately, he wouldn't know where to start to look for him. Besides, he certainly didn't want to initiate any further possibilities for Patricia and Matt to encounter each other.

Patricia had called Dennis, her longtime confidante and friend. He had extended an invitation for her and Robby to stay as long as necessary. She had always sought his opinion in previous times of crisis. She referred to him as her personal guru. He was always the best person to seek sensible advice from. She packed their bags and left for Connecticut.

Robby was excited to see his Uncle Dennis but was so exhausted from the two hour car ride that he immediately fell asleep on the couch. Patricia welcomed the peaceful opportunity to enjoy a cup of coffee with her dear friend. She shared with him her honest feelings about her torn emotions after seeing Matt again.

"Patricia, your feelings of confusion are certainly valid," he agreed. "But let's put things in the proper perspective here. You fell for a guy whom you considered to be your new Prince Charming, which he gave you every reason to believe. You were technically still on the rebound from your divorce from David when you met Matt. He wined and dined you. He made love to you. You went out all the time. You did everything together. You, encouraged by his constant attention, made plans for a future with him. Ultimately, he leaves you without any warning or good-bye. So far am I right?"

"Yes," she mused.

"You later learn that he is not the same man that you were in love with. He has a beautiful wife and daughter who think the world of him, and he has no intention of leaving them for you." Dennis watched Patricia wince at his last words. "I don't mean to hurt you, but you need to be realistic, Patricia."

"I know. Some things are just too hard for me to hear," she sighed. "Go on."

"Seeing him briefly and unexpectedly resurrects all kinds of emotions, because from afar, you can still picture him as your Prince Charming. Up close and in reality he truly is a fictional character and the illusion of your fairy tale can still never come true. The actual reality is that for that one month he lived with you, you were living a fairy tale. You have to let that Prince Charming fade into obscurity because he doesn't really exist. Patricia, you now need to focus on building a future with the real man of your dreams who has proved his devotion to you." Patricia put up her hand to stop Dennis from speaking. He'd said enough already to convince her. David must be hurting so badly right now. David is the man who really did love me back to life and saved me from my delusional obsession of a fantasy. Robby and I probably wouldn't be alive today if it were not for his constant love.

"Oh my God, Dennis, what was I thinking? I can always count on you to be objective. You're truly one of my dearest friends." She reached out to give him a hug.

"Am I still preparing your room?"

"No way, I'm going home to the man I truly love!"

Dennis helped her carry a still sleeping Robby to the car. "Well, that was certainly a short visit. Robby will probably think he was dreaming about being here and seeing me," he laughed.

"Thank you for everything," she said as she blew him a kiss from a partially opened window and drove off.

Dennis called a very depressed David and told him that his family was on their way home. Two hours later David was waiting at the front door anticipating their arrival. He ran from the house as soon as the car pulled up and embraced his wife the second she emerged from the car. Robby was fully awake now but very unsure about the events of the past few hours.

The next morning, Patricia called Katie and asked if they could talk. She needed to reconcile the coincidence with the reality of the circumstances. After Katie walked Laura to school she drove over to the Callahans. David gladly gave her the morning off. He couldn't imagine the pain of betrayal both women must be feeling. He took the day off after his own sleepless night and offered to take Robby out so the women could talk freely.

The women shared their own memories, recalling stories of the Matt they both knew. Patricia confessed that she really thought that she was going to marry Matt and move with him to Hoboken even though he had never asked her. They were so comfortable with each other right from the start. Patricia revealed to Katie how Jack had introduced her that first night at the restaurant to a self-proclaimed 'single' Matt. She admitted inviting him to stay at her house, when she'd learned the bed and breakfast was without electricity. She stressed that he had made the first romantic move toward her.

It was all too surreal for Katie to comprehend Matt as 'the gentleman chameleon' that Patricia described. Katie confirmed Patricia's suspicion that it was she that Matt was calling most mornings outside of Patricia's house while he waited for Jack to pick him up. The two women shared coffee and tears as they put together Matt's puzzle of deception. As for the realization that Matt was Robby's biological father, Patricia insisted Matt never know. She understood it would mean that Laura would never be able to acknowledge Robby as her brother. Katie agreed based on the unpredictable drinking behavior of Matt. She had no intention of hurting the Callahan family who had been so good to her. After their emotional purging they hugged each other and expressed that they couldn't have chosen a better 'other woman.'

MATT'S AMENDS

Katie was deep in thought as she drove to Hoboken to meet Matt. She agreed to have dinner with him when he called her during the week with the intention of confronting him about his Connecticut affair. She clenched her jaw as she thought of his ultimate betrayal. She knew that he thought he had successfully used his gentlemanly wiles of persuading her to meet him. It couldn't have been further from the truth. She wanted closure to this part of her life and was determined to expose his indiscretions and betrayal if he didn't confess them on his own.

Katie believed that Matt was seriously working on his sobriety and that he was working on his Amends Steps. She was well aware of the AA Twelve Steps which were necessary for alcoholics to complete if they were sincere in maintaining their sobriety. She had read the "Big Book" from cover to cover seeking a cure for Matt's affliction long ago. Katie played the Steps back in her head as she drove. Step Eight, yes that was an Amends Step- *"Make a list of all persons we had harmed and became willing to make amends to them all."* And Step Nine was *"Make direct amends to such people wherever possible, except when to do so would injure them or others."* Katie couldn't help wondering if Matt was going to confess his whole sordid affair to her.

And to think that I was horrified when Matt tried to seduce my best friend in my own living room, she mused…and I was disgusted and heartbroken when I found him mugging it out with that floozy in the Irish Bar. But now after learning about his chameleon life with Patricia, I am somehow beyond any emotion. I feel numb. She had been married to a man who she didn't even know! How apropos that Laura had called her pet chameleon Mattie after her daddy. Didn't she say the creature reminded her of Matt? Talk about ironic; she thought her child had sensed his true character better than she.

Oh what am I doing this for? She wasn't worried that seeing him again would rekindle any feelings for him. That spark was extinguished a long time ago. I hope this isn't a big mistake I am making, she said to herself. She hadn't told a soul that she was meeting with him. She didn't want to hear others' opinions of what to say or do. She wanted to handle it her own way. She totally understood Patricia not wanting to see him again, especially to avoid any exposure of the existence of Robby. But Katie didn't spend only one month with Matt. She had been married to this man for 11 years and shared so much with him. She wondered if he had had any other affairs before Patricia. She doubted it. How could he have? We were always together either by ourselves or with Laura, she thought. Our sex life was always good, that can't be the reason he strayed from me…what possibly went wrong between us? She was hoping he was going to put the puzzle together for her.

The ride into Hoboken along the Hudson River was refreshing for Katie. She was glad that she had chosen this scenic route instead of dealing with the chaotic traffic on the New Jersey Turnpike. It brought back wonderful memories for her. The New York skyline had been her visual companion for almost all of her life. She would never have left Hoboken had it not been for Matt and his drinking. She wanted to protect Laura from his drunken antics and broken promises. His sporadic phone calls to her were hard enough to deal with, never mind his unexpected drunken visits to their home. Earlier on, Laura visited Matt on occasion determined to help him conquer his demon of drinking only to come home feeling defeated and helpless. Katie would immediately attend an Al-Anon meeting with her to bring her back to the reality of Matt's disease.

Katie could not believe her luck in finding a parking space on Hudson Street close to where she'd agreed to meet him, near their old apartment. She was glad she wouldn't have to ride around and search for a spot. It was usually a nightmare trying to find a parking space in Hoboken at that time. She could see Matt from her car pacing back and forth in front of the building. He was as handsome as ever, just a lot more weathered from years of abusing his body. What a shame, Katie thought. He was a perfect replica of Adonis to her at one time, her Prince Charming. Now he was a like a fragile man who took a great fall and was trying to put the broken pieces of his life back together again. She wasn't there to help him with that. She was there to get the answer to her biggest question, WHY?

When Matt saw Katie approaching, he smiled with relief. He loved when she wore her long black hair loosely curled as she did now. He admired her from afar; she wore a modest pink blouse and a black knee-length skirt accented with sheer black stockings and heels. He was still very attracted to her. He knew he may never get a chance like this again and reminded himself to proceed with caution. He had always loved Katie and no one else. If it had not been for his alcoholism and his phobia of being alone, he would have never gotten involved with Patricia or Nikki. But how was he going to cleanse his guilt and at the same time explain this underlying fear to her without losing her forever? She would never have agreed to meet him if she didn't still have feelings for him, he convinced himself. The reality of it all was that regardless of anyone else, his sobriety had become more important to him – it meant life or death. The doctor had told him six months ago when he signed into a rehab that if he started drinking again death was imminent. His liver and kidneys could not handle much more abuse. He had been drinking 24/7. He was determined to complete his twelve steps. He reminded himself constantly that he needed to live for Laura. He was hoping to stay sober and re-establish a close and affectionate relationship with her. He knew that would take patience as well as commitment on his part.

They awkwardly kissed each other hello. Even though his lips only brushed her cheek, Katie cringed. "Thank you for coming," he said as he gave her a gentle hug, from which she quickly pulled away. "I really appreciate this," he said with genuine sincerity. Katie gave him a skeptical smile. She felt her stomach tense up, but she knew that she had to stay calm and collected if she was to get relevant answers for his deceitful behavior.

Matt sensed that Katie had her guard up and he couldn't blame her. He knew that his actions from now on had to speak louder than his words. "I made reservations at Gino's.

I remember how you liked it there. It'll be a bit a walk, if you don't mind."

"Of course I don't mind. I've always loved walking around this town. Thank you for remembering that I love that restaurant. It's a very pleasant surprise," Katie coyly lied.

He reminded her of Robby when he used his charm to manipulate in this same way. She smiled at the similarity of their boyish behavior but quickly became somber remembering his betrayal. She had become so attached to and fond of Robby over the last few years that it made it easier to accept him as the result of Matt's deceitful affair.

Matt began to talk as they walked. "I learned a lot about myself in the last few months, Kates. You know that I had a rotten and lonely childhood," he began.

"I heard rumors when we were kids and you alluded to it at times. You always dodged my questions when I asked you any," she answered skeptically.

"That's because I wanted to forget about it. It was a dark, dark time in my life." He sounded very vulnerable.

"Is that why you insisted on Laura always having a night light in her room?" she asked as she thought back on his behavior. "You were very clingy in the dark places especially in bed. Sometimes I couldn't wait until you went to sleep so I could manage to wriggle from under you," she answered as though she were thinking aloud. "Well what about the dark?" she snapped, refraining from being drawn into his spell.

He was taken aback by her response but continued, "When I was young I was terrorized by my babysitter. It was pitch black, suffocating, claustrophobic and inflicted fear like no other," he said, as he instinctively reached for her but she moved out of his reach.

"A babysitter is a WHO not an IT," she responded coldly. She was starting to feel very uncomfortable.

"My babysitter was the IT and IT was a closet," he finally revealed.

"What do you mean?" she asked, softening up a bit.

They reached the restaurant and were seated before he continued. It was a very small intimate restaurant. The dining room was on one side of the paneled half wall and a full bar on the other side. They usually sat at the bar for a drink before moving to their table. Matt managed to reserve their favorite table; Katie decided not to verbally acknowledge that fact.

"My mother couldn't afford a babysitter so she locked me in the closet before she went to work at night," he said matter-of-factly.

"Why didn't you ever mention this before?" she questioned suspiciously. She was sure that he was just trying to gain her sympathy. "Has your drinking made you delusional?"

"At times, but not about this, I didn't tell you because I didn't want you to think that I was weak or damaged. My mother became cold and unaffectionate after my father took off. I guess she resented being left on her own and stuck with me. Why do you think I never went home until late and always spent nights at my friends' homes when I got older?"

The waiter came and took their drink order. Katie wanted a glass of wine to relax, but didn't dare in the company of Matt, so she ordered a club and cranberry and he followed suit. They continued the conversation after the waiter served them their drinks.

"I do remember that. Of course I didn't know why you never wanted to go home. I thought your parents didn't care about you and I felt sorry for you, but weak, no, I never thought that you were weak until you started drinking."

"Katie, do you remember that I always wanted to be with you no matter where you went? And when Laura was born it was the three of us that became inseparable?"

She didn't know where he was going with all of this, but she was losing her patience and becoming very anxious watching him nervously twisting his hands again.

"What does any of this have to do with your amends?" she finally asked him.

"Katie, you asked me once if anything happened while I was on loan in Connecticut," he continued trying to remain calm. "But I did something very mean to you while I was there," he said staring at her intently. "Heaven knows how sorry I am," he said with tears in his eyes.

"Go on," she said with no emotion while she waited for his punch line.

"I was lonely and afraid and... I met someone. Well, it was more like she came on to me really strongly, and I succumbed to her wiles. She was a bit forward." He searched Katie's face for a response but she wore a poker face. She wanted him to confess the whole thing but so far he wasn't taking any responsibility for the affair, claiming it was "the woman's" fault. She wanted to hear more from him.

"Go on," she urged him.

"That's it. I had an affair and I am truly sorry," he added, "Can you forgive me?"

So he wasn't going to tell her everything. She decided to finish the confession for him. She was determined to remain calm and ladylike without reaching over the table and biting his head off. The nerve of him, calling her dear friend "forward", which she knew was a downright lie.

"So this 'tramp', Patricia, took you home with her."

Matt jerked his head alert while holding her gaze. His eyes popped as wide as pumpkins when he heard Patricia's name. He knew he hadn't mentioned it to her.

"You left a couple of small details out. Let's see." Katie went on, "You moved in with her for a month and had incredible sex with her almost every night. Then you called me every day and told me how much you loved and missed me. You even borrowed her car to come home to have sex with me and then you went back to her. You ultimately left her pregnant and without even saying goodbye." Now her face was red but she was determined not to shed one tear in front of him. "I guess you should be sorry! The only thing that kept her alive was Robby – the only good thing you left her with!" She stood up, spit in his face and walked out. Matt was distraught. He was slowly processing her reaction. She hated him. She had already known everything, even about the baby. Wait a minute. She said Robby. Robby! The little boy at Laura's party! I left her with Robby. Patricia never lost the baby, Patricia and David, Katie's friends…David, Katie's boss – it's them! Oh my God! Robby is mine. My son!

Now, he was so desperate for a drink he couldn't wait for the waiter to come over so he ran to the bar and drank until he stumbled out.

Meanwhile, Katie cried as she rushed back to her car. Once inside, her tears of despair became those of liberation and she felt free to finally move on with her life. She completely forgot that she had told Matt about Robby.

THE TRUE GENTLEMAN

Katie's hand trembled as she turned the doorknob to Matt's hospital room. She didn't know what to expect. All she knew was that he was very sick and asked to see her. The nurse who called stressed how very ill he was and that any other family members should also be called but there were none noted on his medical chart. Katie advised her there was no one except for Laura, but she didn't want to alarm her until she could assess the situation. In that case, the nurse said, she would suggest Katie come at once. She hadn't had any contact with Matt in a long while and had no idea what he could want with her. She had given up on him long ago when she found out that their marriage had become a sham. She only wished that he had sought the right help years ago. She would have helped him confront those demons that possessed him. But that was then and now was now.

She quietly entered the dimly lit room and tried to focus on the shadow lying on the bed. She thought that she may have been in the wrong room because the person in the bed appeared to be an elderly, frail and wrinkled man. The only clue to his identity was that the name Matthew Reilly was posted on a nursing board inside his room. The pathetic sight of him brought tears to her eyes. This pitiful, seemingly old man had been a vibrant charming gentleman whom she once had been proud to call her husband. Now he lay attached to intimidating medical contraptions. As she approached the bed, she was sickened to find the shell of the man she once loved so much lying in a restless sleep moaning incoherently. She pulled a chair up close to the bed with the hope that he would soon awaken. He began to stir as though he sensed her presence and began to call for her, "Katie, please…" She couldn't make out the rest of the words he was saying.

She stood and bent closer to him softly speaking, "Matt, it's Katie. I'm here." It was as though he didn't hear at first, then he slowly turned toward her. A sparkle appeared in his eyes as he managed to smile.

He spoke in a very low and weak tone, "Katie, you came. I need your forgiveness. I am so sorry for all the pain I caused you and Laura." He paused. I want you to know you are the only woman…I… have ever loved." Matt stopped speaking, trying to get his breath, but he was determined to finish.

"Matt, it doesn't matter now," Katie began to choke on her words.

"I *need* to make peace with you before it's too late," he pleaded. "I ruined my life with my selfish fears and needs." His voice remained slow and deliberate. "Katie, it wasn't love that I needed from any other woman. It was company." He took a break before he continued. "I couldn't be alone. I never told anyone but you about my mom's abuse," he gasped, really having trouble breathing now.

The tears began to stream down Katie's weary face. "Matt, I would have gone on your business trips with you, had I known your phobia. We could have gone to therapy together." She was now sobbing, "I would have done *anything* for you. I really believed we were both so happy." She dropped her head on his chest as he lifted his hand with much effort to stroke her hair.

"What a mess I've made and I can't take anything back now, only tell you how very sorry I am," he sniveled. Gasping again he said, "Katie, I need to see Patricia. She was also an innocent victim. Do you think Laura would come see me? And can I see the little boy too?" he asked quickly in a desperate plea.

"I'll see what I can do," Katie said, drained. "I think you need your rest, Matt." She lifted her head from his chest and tried to compose herself.

"Kates, thanks for coming to see me. Please understand and know that I will always love you," he insisted. Now the tears ran freely down the side of his face.

Katie managed to muster a smile at the use of his pet name for her and replied, "And I will always love *that* Matt I married years ago." She kissed his cheek. She left his room but once outside she broke down uncontrollably sobbing for what could have been, but now would never be.

She drove home through a torrent of tears as she focused on the good memories she shared with Matt. Like the time she rescued him from drowning in the Hudson River when he slipped and fell and couldn't swim. The two emerged from the water like two wet rats. They shared wonderful times with Ann Marie and Rory. She had to pull over when she thought about their fairy-tale Cinderella wedding with a horse drawn coach and all. Matt had been her Prince Charming.

Her best memory was when Laura was born with Matt present. He cried as he held her in his arms as he whispered over and over, "she'll never be alone." That totally made sense to Katie now after Matt's confession about his fear of abandonment and being alone. If only he had shared his phobia with her earlier, she would have gotten him to seek help. She meant it when she told him that she would have done anything for him. Didn't she go to AA meetings with him? If only he had stayed and worked the program. He waited too long to make his amends. She wouldn't have ever forgiven him, especially after she had become friends with Patricia. She had finally come to the conclusion that he was like a tortured soul, and that she could never have saved him. Alcoholism, that horrible affliction, how it had destroyed her family! She dried her eyes and tried to focus on how she was going to prepare Laura for her last visit with her father.

Patricia felt very skeptical about visiting Matt on his death-bed. He didn't deserve her sympathy after the way he had treated her. Her suppressed emotions began to surface in an eruption. Who did he think he was! Walking back into her life and disrupting it all over again. He could care less that he had left her broken – body and soul. She suffered so much to put her life back together and was not going to let him ruin it. She was so happy with David and Robby. She was finally living a once dreamt fairy tale. As she thought about Robby, her anger for Matt slowly turned to sympathy. Ironically it was Matt who had indirectly given her life back to her and now he was suffering. She was always amazed at the amount of alcohol he drank without it ever affecting his behavior. He would drink vodka like water; he used to keep his stamina, even jumping out of bed in the morning without a hangover after a long night of indulgence. It finally caught up with him, and now he didn't have time to put his life back together. Patricia wrestled with her conflicting feelings about Matt for hours before agreeing to visit him. She realized that she needed to forgive him in person. She wanted to purge the residual bitterness that she still harbored against him. She wanted to be truly free of his emotional hold on her.

"I had no choice but to forgive you, Matt. I refused to surrender my life to an abyss of darkness and anger. I needed every bit of energy to heal my body and couldn't afford to use any of it on hate or regret. You gave David and me the greatest gift of our lives, our son. I choose to remember you as that charming gentleman that swept me off my feet and nothing more. There was something I read in an email once and have always held onto, "*Every relationship is for a reason, a season, or a lifetime.* Robby *was* the reason."

"Thank you for your forgiveness," he sincerely whispered. "Can I please see the boy?" he asked.

"Yes, I've decided that I will let you see him. He's outside with Laura, Katie and David." She went out of the room for a few minutes.

The door reopened and the children entered the room holding tightly to each other's hands as Katie, Patricia and David followed. Katie and Patricia took their places on each side of Matt's bed and David stood at the foot. As they approached the bed, Laura broke loose and threw herself on Matt's chest sobbing, "Oh Daddy, don't leave me. Mommy and I will take you home and help you get better. It'll be just like before; we'll be so happy again. Please Daddy, don't die!"

Matt tried to be as strong as possible as he feebly embraced her. "I love you, princess, and I will always be with you. Every time you think...of your favorite things, think of me...That way I'll never...ever...leave you, honey."

Robby, wide-eyed and concerned about Laura, climbed up on the bed, and innocently said, "Laura, don't cry," as he began to pat her back with his little hand. He turned his attention toward Matt, "Laura isn't your princess, she's my girlfriend," he said adamantly, bringing a smile to Matt's face.

"She's a beautiful girlfriend, isn't she?"

"Uh-huh, I'm gonna marry her when I grow up," the little boy announced.

Matt was slowly stroking Laura's hair but his breathing had become more laborious. Talking was even harder, but he was determined to stay as long as he could.

Laura lifted her head and smiled, "Daddy, isn't he the cutest little boy you've ever seen?"

Matt had been intently watching Robby. "He sure is." Matt couldn't help seeing the child's resemblance to Laura and himself. "Can I have a hug, Robby?" Matt asked smiling.

Trying to follow Laura's behavior he crawled up on the other side of Matt, lifted his head and gave Matt a big hug followed by a kiss on the cheek.

Matt kissed the top of Robby's head. Matt was now holding both of his children in his arms. He leaned his head on Robby's and whispered, "I hope you grow up to be a real gentleman like your father." As he said this, he looked straight at David. Then Matt closed his eyes for the last time and his arms fell to the bed as he drew his final breath.

EPILOGUE

Katie and Ann Marie sat on the stoop of Katie's parents' home watching Laura, Suzie and Robby playing hopscotch on the sidewalk. It's like **Déjà** vu isn't it," Ann Marie offered. That was us a lifetime ago."

"It was a wonderful lifetime," replied Katie. We did have a great childhood. That's why it was so important for me to move Laura back here to Hoboken."

"Did you ever picture us both back here living in our parents' homes?" asked Ann Marie.

"No, but I couldn't be happier. I liked Cedar Grove very much and it was so close to work for me, but this is where I belong. The Hudson waterfront is in my blood. Anyway, I'll still visit Cedar Grove on my frequent visits to Patricia and David."

"Katie, do you ever think you and Patricia will ever tell the kids that they're related?"

"We've decided not to unless there is some unforeseen reason or at least until they are both grown. We intend to always keep them close and we have no intention of destroying Laura's ideal image of her perfect father. You know, it's funny the way people can be immortalized through children's selective memory."

"Matt and Laura had a very special relationship. They were so sweet together," Ann Marie admitted.

"Sometimes it was hard to know who the adult was and who the child was," Katie smiled wistfully, remembering the good times.

"So, how is everything with you and Jack?" Ann Marie tried to turn the conversation.

"Great! However I'm taking it slow. I've fallen for a gentleman before. This time I want to be more aware of myself. Remember, I already had my Prince Charming. It seems, though, that I kissed a chameleon and not a frog. I think I need to get my reptiles and amphibians straight," Katie quipped.

Ann Marie laughed at the thought. "You never know, this time maybe we'll have a double wedding."

"We'll see. Only time will tell...for now let's have some fun," Katie said, standing, and gently tugging Ann Marie's arm to join her.

Patricia and David were amused when they pulled up to the house to find Katie and Ann Marie having the time of their lives playing hopscotch with the three kids. Sometimes, it seems, there really can be a different kind of happily-ever-after.

J. B. Kelly resides in New Jersey and is retired from a major communications corporation after thirty years. She held a second job as a waitress for twenty-eight of those years. Her son is a successful spinal surgeon and raising him is what J. B. considers to be her greatest accomplishment. Kelly loves travelling, reading, and Broadway shows. This is her second book, a sequel to *The Gentleman Chameleon*. Her third novel, *The Prism Window*, which delves into the murder mystery genre, will both stun and surprise her many fans!